BEN FRANKLIN AND THE CHAMBER OF TIME

CHRIS HEIMERDINGER

BEN FRANKLIN AND THE CHAMBER OF TIME

Maasai Publishing
Provo, Utah

Cover design by Douglass Cole, Orem, Utah
Prepared for printing by Brian Carter / www.SunriseBooks.com

Originally published by Deseret Book Company.

For my wife, Beth,
who patiently improved it.

Special thanks to Ms. Claude-Anne Lopez of Yale University
for her detailed review for historical accuracy.

CHAPTER 1

The lightning flash pierced through, around, and under the lids of Benjamin Franklin's sleeping eyes. He opened them abruptly and steadied his gaze on the unlatched window. The morning sunlight had been subdued by a shield of roiling gray clouds, advancing from the east. The memories of a thousand similar scenes were set loose in Franklin's mind, swarming about like fireflies. He caught his next breath, held it in his lungs. His fingers gripped the bed sheet. Counting: two seconds, three, four, five—at last came the accompanying crack of thunder. This coincided with a stab of pain, and Franklin let the air escape his lungs in a slow, rasping exhale. Even a subtle thing like anticipation inflamed the tenderness in his chest. Ten days earlier, an attack of pleurisy had sent him to his sickbed. The bed might as well have been a coffin. The infection had dealt him a crippling blow, rendering him unable to rise or stand.

As another lightning bolt illuminated the interior of his bedroom, the philosopher's heart was swept up in the nostalgia of younger, more exuberant days—days that a man of eighty-four years is wont to remember. He glanced at the picture his nurse had balanced at the foot of his bed. The yellowed and faded print of the *Day of Judgment* had been

CHRIS HEIMERDINGER

stored in a dusty garret for many years. A few days earlier, a fateful whim had inspired him to have it placed where it was permanently within his view.

But despite the pain in his chest, despite the onerous theme of the painting, and despite the pessimistic expectations of family and physicians, Franklin felt an invigoration in his muscles that he hadn't known for over a week. The flicker of lightning convinced him that now, perhaps, he could try to stand. Maybe even walk. The plain truth was, he *had* to stand. He had to walk. If he wanted to live, this might be his last opportunity.

The door opened. In stepped his only daughter, Sally. During those periods of the last two years when sickness had confined Franklin to his bed, Sally had proven a most attentive and loving nurse. She carried in with her a glass of Madeira, whose narcotic effect had been magnified with opiates. Franklin cringed. He loathed his dependence on laudanum, certain that his use of it over the last two years had actually *aided* in the deterioration of his body, leaving him a withered and emaciated husk. But opium was the only defense doctors could give him against the mounting pains—pleurisy, gout, and the rest.

Sally was pleased to see her father's eyes open. For several days now his moments of full coherency had been rare.

"You're awake," she said affectionately. "You look very much better today." After setting the drink on the night table, she noticed the window drapes fluttering in expectation of the coming storm. She shut the window, bolted it, and then returned to her father's bedside. "Even your cough finally seems to have disappeared."

Sally's smile turned down slightly as she felt Franklin's forehead. The fever still burned. Nevertheless, she spoke

2

words of encouragement. "Before long you will be fully recovered."

Sally took up the wine glass and lifted her father's head to help him drink. Franklin raised his hand to protest.

Surprised, Sally inquired, "Has the pain also subsided?"

"No," said Franklin. "But I wish to be clear today."

Sally winced a little. Administering wine and laudanum comforted *her* nearly as much as it comforted *him.* Watching her father groan and cry wrenched at Sally's heart. She nearly became insistent, but the conviction in her father's voice told her it was futile.

"Everyone has finished a lovely breakfast. Do you wish me to carry a tray up to you?"

Franklin shook his head. "What is the date today?"

"April seventeenth," Sally answered. Then she smiled and teased, "Why do you wish to know? Were you planning a picnic? The weather is hardly permitting."

"No," Franklin replied. But he did not tell her his reason for asking. Actually, Benjamin Franklin wanted to know the date of the day he would die.

Or might April seventeenth of the year 1790 be known as the day I am reborn and renewed?

His thought had no particular spiritual relevance. Franklin's belief in an afterlife was sincere, even if he had yet to subscribe to the tenets of any particular sect. And, indeed, he felt that passing from this life to the next must certainly involve some kind of rebirth and renewal. But at this instant he had something else in mind.

"I wish to rise from my bed," Franklin told his daughter.

Sally filled with excitement and apprehension. "Do you feel strong enough?"

"I want to rise," clarified Franklin, "so that my bed might be made up. I wish to die in a decent manner."

3

Sally was crestfallen. She knew her father was very ill. Two days earlier Dr. Jones had voiced grave predictions. Still, she'd witnessed her father triumph over countless obstacles, public and private, physical and emotional. She knew he was not infallible; from time to time he was even given to complain, agonize, weep, even misjudge. But never had she seen him give up the fight.

For now Sally chose to ignore her father's statement, assisting him in his painful struggle to sit up. She moved the covers off his legs so he could maneuver them out onto the floor. At last, she choked down the emotion in her voice and said cheerfully, "Now, you mustn't say such things. You *will* recover. No doubt you will be with us for many years longer."

For a lingering moment, Franklin did not respond. He sat there on his bed, gaping at the floor. Then he calmly replied, "I hope not."

Sally pretended she hadn't heard him and began to remove the pillows from his bed. "Perhaps if you slept more on your side," she advised, "you might breathe a little easier."

"A dying man can do nothing easily."

Sally might not have considered these statements so blunt and calloused if she had heard *all* her father's thoughts. Franklin had no desire to continue living if his only relief was to be found in narcotics that muddled his mind and suffocated his spirit. Death was not an unwelcome prospect for Benjamin Franklin. Like every man since the dawn of time, Franklin had frequently contemplated the mysteries that awaited him beyond this mortal coil. As a sprightly and optimistic man of middle-age he'd even written the epitaph for his own tombstone, looking to the day when the "work" known as Benjamin Franklin would appear once more in a new and more perfect edition, corrected and amended by its Almighty Author.

But there was something in the nature of man, something ingrained in the fiber of his most primeval instincts, which decreed that if it were possible to forestall that journey called death, he was plainly obligated to do it. Battling forces which others called natural fate had been the lot of Franklin's life. He remembered particularly the year he introduced his lightning rod to the world. Many had condemned the Philadelphia philosopher. They said that tampering with the will of Providence would incur Heaven's just wrath. And, in fact, when an earthquake struck Boston in 1755, one clergyman blamed the entire occurrence on the citizens of that city who were defying divine will by erecting upon their houses those "works of the devil" known as lightning rods.

In Franklin's mind there existed one scant possibility— implausible as it might have seemed to anyone of sober thinking—that he might yet stay the clammy hand of death. He was, therefore, obligated to make the attempt. Franklin might have submitted himself to this task two years earlier, but that same primal fear which urges a man to survive had also urged him to procrastinate. Now he could procrastinate no longer. Within hours he was certain he'd be dead.

Another flash of lightning crossed the sky. A crack of thunder followed. The storm was much closer now. It was time.

"Benny," Franklin uttered absently. "Where is Benny?"

"Benjamin is downstairs," Sally replied. "Do you wish me to send him up? Would you like him to help you walk?"

"Yes," said Franklin.

After Sally went to fetch her oldest son, Franklin put his hand to his chest. The pain was excruciating. So hard to breathe. Every intake of air took increasing effort. Franklin feared it might be too late already. It was all he could do to keep from fainting. The journey he was about to ask his grandson to help him make was all the way down two flights of stairs, along the hallway of the main floor, and into the locked study where he had stored all of his electrical apparatus. It was an unthinkable distance for someone in his condition. But this was the journey he had to make, for there in the room's dusty darkness, toward the farthest corner, sat the final and most dangerous invention of his career.

The seed of the notion that became this invention had gestated in Franklin's mind for nine years before he began its construction. Finally, in 1787, with the help of his grandson, Benny, he set out to make a prototype. Franklin could trace the beginnings of this idea back to a private conversation he'd had with the philosopher Voltaire at the Academy of Sciences in Paris in 1778. Voltaire was then eighty-four years old—the same age as Franklin now. The question that the Frenchman had put to Franklin went as follows: "In all your years of experimentation, have you ever discovered some property about electricity that made it possible to rejuvenate the vitality of human flesh and bone?"

Voltaire conceded that in its most common form electricity was one of nature's most destructive forces; nevertheless, he nurtured a pet idea that one might divide the various properties of a lightning bolt, just as one might peel the skin from a piece of fruit, and discover within a fiber of this fiery fluid the essence of life itself.

Franklin greatly sympathized with the philosopher's question. He was himself seventy-five at that time. It was easy to understand how an aging man could engross himself in such speculations. But he had to reply in the negative. Although he was aware that in England and elsewhere doctors had performed experiments to see if electricity might relieve the effects of paralysis, palsy, and deafness, positive effects were either absent or temporary. The only permanent improvements Franklin had ever observed occurred when he had personally treated a woman suffering from violent convulsions. The woman, on the verge of suicide, had come to Franklin as a final resort. Three and a half months of shock therapy had utterly cured her. But this was hardly the kind of sweeping rejuvenation to which Voltaire referred. Disappointed, and perhaps slightly embarrassed to have asked, Voltaire dropped the subject.

And this is where the issue rested until a dinner party at Franklin's French residence at Passy six years later. Among the guests that evening, besides the ever-congenial Thomas Jefferson, was the French scientist Abbé Guillaume Raynal. The Abbé supported the theory that animals—and even men!—degenerated in the New World, were smaller in stature, and by implication were weaker in intellect. After listening to such bunk for a period of minutes Franklin decided to settle the matter once and for all. On one side of the table sat all of the Americans, including William Carmichael and David Humphreys, both burly six-footers. On the other side sat the Frenchmen. Franklin, with his imposing bulk, stood up and had everyone else do the same to see on which side of the table nature had degenerated. By comparison, the Frenchmen appeared remarkably diminutive. The Abbé himself was a mere shrimp.

The incident gave Franklin a chuckle even hours later that evening as he retired to his bed. Before falling asleep, his train of thought drifted to a recent fad in Paris which centered on the theories of Dr. Franz Mesmer. Mesmer believed that all the ills of humanity could be cured by the action of a universal fluid found throughout nature and commonly referred to as "animal magnetism." Although Franklin had done much to dispel this fad and expose Mesmer as a charlatan, he couldn't help but wonder if Mesmer had not touched upon a matter that deserved further exploration. Might physical transformations be possible as a result of continuous exposure to a certain climate, as suggested by Raynal, or some mystical force, as suggested by Mesmer? Not a dubious force like animal magnetism, but a much more universal power, like electricity? Within a short time Franklin was also recalling the question posed to him six years earlier by Voltaire. All at once an image popped into his mind, an image of an apparatus that might indeed divide the properties of electricity, if in fact such a division were possible.

The end result of this revelation was the contraption which now sat behind the locked door of the room where Franklin stored all of his electrical equipment. He had actually pondered the matter another full year before he began its construction. By then it was 1786 and the Continental Congress had brought him home to America. It was still another year before he could give the matter his full attention, after the business of the Constitutional Convention concluded in September. And then, with his grandson Benjamin Franklin Bache performing most of the physical labor of running to and fro from the iron and silversmiths and erecting no less than six lightning rods in a most unusual configuration, the "chamber," as Franklin referred to it (or "torture chamber" as Benny was wont to call it), was finally completed—though far from perfected.

When the next thunderstorm enshrouded Philadelphia, Franklin and Benny chose as their first subject for the chamber an old family rooster. The rooster was promptly burnt to a crisp.

Not to be defeated, Franklin awaited the next storm and placed within the chamber several dozen cockroaches. After the rods had attracted a healthy spark, Franklin and Benny returned to find the chamber completely empty. From the foul smell that pervaded the room, Franklin was left to conclude that the roaches had entirely disintegrated.

Franklin directed Benny to make a few minor adjustments, but overall he felt disheartened about the whole affair and asked Benny if he wouldn't mind keeping the matter under his hat for the present. Franklin started to conclude he was just too old and feeble to give the project the kind of self-discipline it required.

Nevertheless, in March of 1788, as another thunderstorm began brewing on the horizon, Franklin and Benny decided to test the invention on an old, enfeebled stray cat that everyone in the neighborhood had unkindly christened Scat. Scat's spine and limbs were so afflicted with arthritis that it shrieked with agony the instant it was touched.

The subsequent lightning bolt that Franklin's chamber attracted was one of the most powerful he had ever drawn from heaven. The cat was not killed, but neither was it conscious. It lay in a kind of coma state for a full night and a day. And then, about seven o'clock the following evening, Benny excitedly interrupted a meeting of the American Philosophical Society that was being conducted in Franklin's dining room. He whispered in his grandfather's ear that Scat was awake and purring. Franklin promptly adjourned the meeting to attend to a "family emergency."

The cat's arthritis was gone! Its bedraggled and misshapen appearance had given way to a limber feline physique. Its body was exactly that of a strong and healthy cat in its prime.

Franklin hastily prepared his notes for a bold announcement to the world, and hinted to several friends that he had tapped the "fountain of youth." But precisely four days after the cat's apparent rejuvenation, it began to show signs of its age once again. The disfiguring symptoms of arthritis returned. Seven days after emerging from the chamber, Scat the cat died. Like most other medical applications of electricity, the apparent benefits were only temporary. For the time being, Franklin placed his notes in Benny's possession and awaited the next storm.

Franklin felt inspired to direct one final adjustment on the chamber. The next two storms, however, failed to draw any spark from the lightning. Shortly thereafter, his health seriously deteriorated and he became confined to his bed or his bedroom the majority of the time. Benny, who had recently graduated from college, was just beginning his career as a printer and found less and less time to dabble in his grandfather's contraptions. Instead, he spent any spare time he found for his grandfather writing letters at Franklin's dictation as well as helping him to add a few final pages to his memoirs. By now, the chamber had undoubtedly gathered a thick layer of dust.

Franklin looked toward the window as another flash of lightning streaked the sky. The storm was now upon them. Rain began pelting the glass. Benny appeared in the doorway.

"Grand Papa? You called for me?"

"Yes, my boy," he said weakly.

"Do you wish to dictate a letter?"

Franklin shook his head. "I wish to go to my study."

"Which study is that?"

Franklin's shaky hand reached into the tiny drawer in his night table. He felt around, and then he drew out the key that had sat there for two years. Franklin gazed squarely at

Benny for several moments. Benny swallowed hard. He realized now which study his grandfather meant. Benny glanced out at the storm, and then back at Franklin.

"What is it that you plan to do?"

Franklin raised his chin in resolve. "I plan to sleep in the chamber."

"But that's madness, Grand Papa! You could be electrocuted—roasted to a crisp! Do you not remember the rooster?"

"Please," Franklin interrupted. "Listen to me, Benny. In either case, before this day is over, I will be dead."

"But—"

"*Please,*" Franklin repeated, closing his eyes to block out the pain.

Benny rarely refused his grandfather. Mechanically, he went over to the bed. As he lifted Franklin's arm and put it around his neck, he thought, *I will take him there, but I will never let him go through with this madness.* Franklin gasped in pain as Benny stood him up. Benny realized how light his grandfather had become.

"I think it will be easier, Grand Papa, if I just carry you."

Before Franklin could protest, Benny lifted the fragile old man into his arms. For a moment, Franklin lost consciousness. When he awoke, Benny had already carried him down the first flight of stairs and had begun descending the second. Franklin had managed to retain the key in his grip.

Two of Franklin's younger grandchildren, Deborah and Richard Jr., came bounding up the stairs. Little Debbie noted briefly to Richard that Grand Papa was out of his room; then they scurried on about their business, oblivious to what may have been happening, as children of nine and six years are apt to be. Franklin felt his heart constrict a little. It might be the last time he would see his grandchildren run and play.

On the other hand, if it were possible to see his progeny grow just a little older, that alone made this endeavor worth the attempt.

There were several people still in the dining room as they reached the main floor. Benny did not draw their attention. He disappeared with his grandfather into the hallway and toward the study.

When they reached the locked room, Franklin requested that Benny set him down in the chair just outside the door. Although he'd been carried, Franklin felt greatly fatigued by the trip. After a fit of low coughing, he reached toward his grandson. Benny leaned down.

"Whatever may happen," whispered Franklin, "if I am killed or otherwise rendered unable to communicate, I want you to promise me that you will not reveal the intended purpose of this chamber for fully ten years. Do you promise me?"

Benny looked perplexed. "Yes, of course, Grand Papa. But why would you make such a request?"

Franklin thought a moment. "For the sake of my family, I would have the world speak of my more respectable accomplishments for a period of time, rather than have my detractors tarnish my good name with the report that I spent my final years dabbling in the vainest sort of alchemy."

Franklin wasn't sure if his shaky hand could work the key in the lock. He tried to hand it to Benny.

Benny stared down at it, his mouth hanging open. He began reaching out to take it and then abruptly changed his mind.

"I can no longer be a party to this, Grand Papa!"

As Benny fled down the hall, Franklin looked toward the locked doorway.

Benny burst into the dining room, where he found

William Temple, Franklin's grandchild on his son's side, and Polly Hewson, the visiting daughter of Franklin's landlady in England.

"Where is my mother?" Benny asked.

"I believe she's down in the kitchen," reported Polly.

The kitchen was in the cellar. Benny descended the stairway and found her scrubbing the breakfast dishes. He might have wondered why the maid was not helping her, but then Benny noticed she had been crying. He knew his mother liked to work when she was upset. Apparently Sally's short conversation with her father had been disturbing.

"Mama," said Benny. "You must come with me to talk some sense into him."

Sally shook off her gloomy countenance. "Who? Your grandfather?"

"Yes," said Benny. "He's talking quite foolishly. I carried him down from his room and—"

"You did what? Where is he!"

"In the hall, just down from the library." Benny followed his mother up the stairs. "He's plainly convinced that he is going to die today."

Sally marched through the dining room. Polly and William looked to Benny for an explanation, but Benny ignored them and kept on his mother's heel. Polly and William decided they had better follow.

As Benny crossed before the front door, he happened to glance at the window. The rain now fell in sheets. He heard an awesome peal of thunder. Upon reaching the hallway, Benny was surprised to see that the study door had been unlocked. It stood open, revealing a dark and dusty entrance. His grandfather had managed to get it open after all.

Suddenly the hallway ignited under a blinding flash of the whitest, purest light any of them had ever seen. The apparent explosion had come from within the study. The four adults shrieked in astonishment and shielded their eyes.

The light froze everyone in their tracks, except for Benny. Desperately, he pushed his way past his mother until he stood in the doorway. *Please no, please no!* clamored in his brain.

Benny caught hold of the paneling around the doorway and peered into the room. A cloud of vapor obscured his view of the chamber. The odor within was most foul and putrid. After a moment, the vapor lifted. Benny dropped to his knees. He hung his head and muttered under his breath, *Just like the cockroaches.*

The chamber was empty. Benjamin Franklin was gone.

CHAPTER 2

Franklin, too, felt the blast of light as the lightning struck the rods atop his chamber. He pinched shut his eyes and gritted his teeth. Immediately, Franklin felt as if he were floating, hovering. And yet he felt the most unusual trembling throughout his body, as if every drop of blood in his veins had started to boil. Waves of intense heat and bitter cold washed over his flesh so rapidly that his mind had little time to register one condition or the other. Franklin pressed both of his ears. The pressure was enormous. He thought his eardrums might burst. But at no single moment during this transformation did Benjamin Franklin lose consciousness.

Bravely, he opened his eyes, knowing full well that another blast of light might leave him permanently blind. As he tried to focus, he saw new lights above, below, and all around him, not so bright as ill-defined. Every conceivable color in the spectrum circled him like an angry swarm of bats. The colors blurred and blended, swept in one direction, then the other, and then a hundred different directions at once.

Again Franklin felt as if he were floating, and yet his body was obviously supported. There *was* a surface. He could touch it, sense it, feel its continually shifting contours. Franklin watched his legs, arms, and hips involuntarily rise and fall, adjusting somehow to a surface in continual

15

metamorphosis. Franklin had the distinct impression that he was in transit, moving lambently along the contours of this surface like a sheet of silk along a stairway, ever molding to the shapes over which it is dragged. But was it Franklin in motion, or did the surface move beneath him while he remained firmly in place?

Franklin wondered if he were hallucinating. Hallucinations were a common side effect of the opiates he took for pain. But he had not taken any opiates that day. Was this some sort of relapse? With every breath he smelled a different odor, sweet like tree sap or fresh like an Atlantic wind, acrid like a swamp or putrid like rotting beef. Effortlessly, Franklin's body continued to rise and fall, twist and tumble.

At last there came a violent impact, like a hammer on an anvil. The wind expelled from his lungs, as if he'd run full force into a stone wall. His body literally bounced into the air. Franklin thought his frail bones would shatter as he landed. He hit the ground with a grunt, but by some miracle he had not been harmed. The strangely alternating ground had acted as a cushion.

Franklin felt no sense of location. He couldn't begin to fathom what was happening. Instantly the colors all around him scattered like a shoal of fish. For a fragment of time there was only blackness, and then the light rushed back and he began to perceive shapes all around him—trees, grass, sky, clouds, and the yellow sun. But the images would not sit still. They vibrated. For a split second the sun seemed to settle in the center of the sky—and then it began to move— *backwards!*

The yellow sphere whipped across the heavens in the wrong direction like the dart of a hummingbird. The sun was followed by the moon, also spinning with backwards momentum. The two planetary bodies chased each other like a pair of playful sparrows. Night and day flashed on and off with increasing velocity. The sun and moon were soon perceptible only as bright streaks across the sky. And then the colors smeared and blended again. Franklin felt the earth rolling beneath his back, its contours shifting and reforming. Again he felt the boiling in his blood and the waves of hot and cold.

After a moment, Franklin perceived the sun and moon again. The velocity appeared to be decreasing. The landscape around him steadily fell back into focus. The sun came to a full stop in the center of a cold grey sky.

But where am I? There was snow and ice all around him! He could hear the roar of a waterfall. *What is happening to me?* This hallucination didn't compare with any he'd experienced under laudanum. A bitter wind blew through Franklin's thin nightgown. In mere moments he would be frozen solid! His muscles ached more than he'd ever remembered, even after enduring the most strenuous labor. Yet in spite of the stiffness—in spite of his enfeebling illness and age—Franklin marveled to discover that he had the strength to stand.

But Franklin had scarcely pushed himself up on one knee when the sun began moving again. Only now it was moving forward! It was as if the world had paused only long enough to gain the momentum to spin in the other direction. Franklin felt like an arrow shot into the trunk of a tree only to have the shaft quiver violently until it settled into place. The moon began chasing the sun again. The colors blurred and blended. In spite of the shifting contours of the earth, Franklin kept his balance. It was like standing in a skiff during an ocean storm. Franklin managed to straighten his back as the velocity of the whirling sun and moon diminished once again.

When the spinning stopped, it was no longer winter. The leaves were green. The roar of the waterfall was replaced by hundreds of cheering voices. He appeared to have materialized in the middle of a park or garden. A red ribbon settled on his shoulder. Confetti rained in his hair. Hundreds of people all around him carried signs and banners: "Mickelson for President!" "Your Home Town Supports You!" and "Mickelson—Perfect Vision for 2020!"

The people didn't seem to notice him at all, yet one gentleman stood close enough that Franklin might have touched him. Perhaps in all the hoopla the appearance of an oddly dressed old man could be easily ignored. Franklin's feet were planted between two metal rails. A short distance up the rails stretched an impressively long implement of transportation; it looked like a caravan of wagons all hooked together. On the sides of this machine hung more banners: "Victory on Tuesday" and "Nonstop to the White House." A man, a woman, and two children stood at the head of the nearest wagon in the caravan, waving enthusiastically to the crowd. Franklin decided this man must be the presidential candidate, along with his wife and children. But over what state or nation was this man vying to be president? It couldn't be America. This place did not even remotely resemble the America Franklin knew.

A few scant seconds—that's all the time Franklin had to absorb his surroundings before the world started spinning backwards again. The crowd disappeared. The sun and moon began their familiar chase. Franklin watched as the leaves on the trees shriveled and then disappeared, leaving skeletal branches throughout the park. And then all the colors smeared. The ground began shifting.

When the spinning halted, Franklin stood near the river again. It was cold, but not as cold as before. Franklin realized he stood near the edge of a cliff! One sideways step would have sent him plunging twenty feet into the swift-flowing waters. The duration of time before the moon and sun began chasing each other again—forward this time—seemed shorter than before.

When the world stopped, the moon was positioned in the center of the heavens. It was night. Some sort of lanterns or lights illuminated the area. Franklin stood between two rails again, but the landscape no longer looked much like a park. The trees looked smaller. Some looked as though they'd shifted to different positions.

A deafening roar filled Franklin's ears, further amplified by the blast of a horn. Franklin turned on his heel. Terror filled his breast. A menacing black mass barreled towards him. At the head of this mass blazed a terrible white light. The mass was upon him. There was no escape! Franklin shielded his face.

But he wasn't crushed. Franklin lowered his arms. The landscape was spinning again. Vertigo caused Franklin to drop down on his hands. When he raised his eyes, he found himself nestled in a field of wheat. A dozen yards away crawled the queerest looking contraption he'd ever seen, somehow cutting or processing the wheat. Franklin looked about to see if he was anywhere near his previous locations. There appeared to be the outline of a river a half mile away. Franklin suspected he was remaining within one general vicinity, but there were no hints as to what vicinity it was. The sun jolted in the other direction. The contraption disappeared. The golden wheat field began to smear.

During the next interstice, Franklin found himself back near the cliffs that overlooked the river. Above him there now stood a bridge and, beyond the bridge, a man-made waterfall. Directly under the bridge stretched a pipe of some sort, less than a foot in diameter. Franklin caught sight of a young boy, twelve or thirteen years old, out in the middle of this pipe, clinging for dear life. What in heaven's name was he doing out there? How could he possibly have crawled out so far without slipping? Franklin got a clear look at the boy's face. Wild panic raged in the child's eyes.

And then the boy let go! In horror, Franklin watched as the adolescent plunged into the churning waters, his arms flailing once before the river sucked him under. Franklin's gaze remained transfixed on the spot where the boy had disappeared. In vain he pleaded to understand: *Why? Why have I witnessed this horrible event?*

Before Franklin had stomached the shock, the sun whipped back and the landscape smeared. The pauses between each backward and forward jolt were considerably shorter, as if the arrow's quivering shaft was finally settling in the middle. For an instant Franklin found himself back near the park, during a drenching downpour. Then back near the bridge. Then crouched in deep snow. It was day and then night. Summer and then winter. There were clouds and then stars. Each time his ground position changed, but toward the last it varied in each instance by only a couple of yards. At the very end there was no pause for reverse momentum at all, just a sharp jolting back and forth. The sun and moon couldn't decide whether to go forward or back. The quivering intensified. Franklin saw multiple images of the sun and moon. The images vibrated together. Franklin sickened with vertigo. His tongue pressed against the back of his throat. His eyes rolled back in his head. Finally he collapsed.

A perfect, dreamless sleep overcame the Philadelphia philosopher. He was completely unaware of any passage of time, forward or backward. When his eyelids fluttered open, it was night. Stars glimmered above. Ripe-smelling blades of grass curled over his face. The world was embraced by a remarkable silence. Nothing smeared. Nothing blended. None of the lights or colors twisted or twirled. The universe, time, and space appeared to have settled into place. The astonishing hallucinations were over. The drug-like effects of the chamber had worn off at last. Franklin had made it back to reality.

But what reality was this?

Franklin turned his head slightly to the left and noted the branches of a lofty tree against the night sky. *Outdoors? I'm outdoors! How did I possibly get outside of my house?* And then he realized the season was all wrong. Even in the moonlight he could tell that the oak tree boasted not the nascent buds of April, but the rich, full foliage of summer.

How could it be summer? Unless . . .

Unless summer was the perpetual season of heaven! But if this was heaven, why did his body ache so? He'd thought heaven should, by some tacit obligation, bring an end to the aches and ills of the body. Either heaven was a sphere altogether different from the one described by history's various theologians, or this was not heaven.

A coma? Yes, it seemed entirely probable that after the hallucinations his mind had fallen into a state of limbo. As he slept, he would have been blissfully unaware of any change of season. But why would his comatose body have been left outdoors, abandoned in the weeds?

Franklin raised his right arm. By some muscular illusion, it felt as if the limb broke free from something—as if it had shattered the membrane of an embryonic sac. As he moved his other three limbs, he experienced the same kind of sensation. The soreness melted away, gathering at the center of his spine and then draining into the soft, dark soil beneath his back.

Yet his physical troubles were not over. As Franklin attempted to sit up, he realized the soreness had been replaced by a kind of palsy. It was as if his mind had forgotten how to move, how to sit up, or how to stand. Franklin opened and closed his fists. Then he bent each elbow successively. It was several moments before he felt confident enough to sit up. Moving this way felt very awkward, as if he were operating the body of another individual. Franklin examined his surroundings. He was nestled in a grove of oak trees. The flames of several street lanterns burned at some distance. At least, he *thought* they were street lanterns. The intensity of the light exceeded any he had ever seen in America or Europe.

A walkway lay about five yards to his right. In many ways this place had the same appearance as the park or plaza where that political rally had occurred. So it hadn't been a total hallucination after all. But the park looked different again. Hadn't there been a nice green lawn? The park now looked more like a patch of woods. But what did all this matter? He still had no clues as to how he got here in the first place.

Franklin attempted to stand. The effort was wobbly at best. *I must look like a drunkard,* thought Franklin. Just then, he noticed that he was not alone. To his left stood several persons, looking upon him as some sort of freak. In the dark these people were only silhouettes; he could not make out their faces. One of them pointed him out to the others.

"Look," he said. "A wino!"

The persons, seven young men in all, closed in.

"I could use some help," said Franklin innocently.

"I'll say you could," replied one of the boys. "Didn't anybody tell you this place is off limits to anyone but us after dark?"

Franklin squinted to see if he could make out this person's features. He could only note that the boy's hair had been trimmed in such a way as to give it very sharp edges on top and a uniquely square appearance. "I apologize," said Franklin. "I was not aware of this law."

The boys laughed. They began circling him like wolves. Franklin realized these boys were no more than a gang of ruffians. He'd seen plenty of their kind in the streets of London and Paris.

"Well, maybe we can educate you on some of the finer points of local law. This is *our* turf, and we don't like it when drunks try to weasel in on it."

The boy stepped forward. He kicked Franklin in the stomach! Franklin doubled over, gasping for breath. As he staggered, the boy turned to the others and explained, "That was *mae-geri*. Got it? Everyone say it."

"*Mae-geri*," the other boys mumbled.

"Good! Now this is *mawashi-geri*." The boy delivered a roundhouse kick to Franklin's head.

Franklin went down. *Can't they see I'm over eighty years old?* he wondered. *Have these boys no humanity?*

"Say it. *Mawashi-geri*," demanded the first boy.

"*Mawashi-geri*," mumbled the others.

"If you're gonna learn karate," the first boy told his students, "you gotta learn to say each move in Japanese."

"What's this called?" asked a second boy as he lunged forward and clumsily delivered his own kick.

"I don't think there's a name for that one," said the first boy. "But this is *kakato-geri*." With the heel of his foot, the boy delivered his final blow.

Franklin tasted blood. "Please," he pleaded. "I'm . . . an old man."

"Old?" said the first boy. "If you're old, my grandpa must be Methuselah."

Another gang member stepped forward to add one last kick, but the first boy stopped him. "Save it," he insisted, "for something useful." The boy turned back to Franklin. "I'd advise you to sleep it off at the shelter from now on. Capisce?"

The ruffians left Franklin splayed in the grass, bruised and bleeding. He rolled onto his back. The heavens were blurry. He uttered a silent prayer before his injuries and the atrophy in his muscles caused him to black out again.

Powerful Goodness, if this is a dream, I pray I might awaken. If I am awake, I pray I might understand. If this be neither of these states, I pray that I might, in peace, die.

CHAPTER 3

Franklin was certain now that the visions which came and went were only dreams. Yet the dreams were so unusual, so out of sync, like those that accompany a high fever. An image of his father transformed into that of his son, William. His brother James became his nephew Jemmy. These familiar faces spoke in strange, unmatching voices—William chided him in the droning chant of Lord North, the British prime minister, while his nephew pouted in a voice like that of John Adams of Massachusetts. Franklin relived a nightmare that hadn't afflicted him for over seventy years—the drowning of his sixteen-month-old brother Ebenezer in a tub of suds. It was an event he had never witnessed, since it occurred before he was born, but the image had been impressed most vividly by his mother. Likely it had been dredged up by the hallucination of the boy who drowned in the river. Just as Franklin started coming to, he heard the voice of his wife, Deborah, sixteen years dead, calling out to him as if from a cold, dark hollow, "Come home, my dear child. Come home. Come home . . . "

Franklin opened his eyes. He still lay in the wooded park, but it was daylight now. A glance at the sun said it was late afternoon. He had slept much longer than he might have guessed.

The bruises he had received the night before still pained

him, but Franklin was surprised to discover that the awkwardness that had made it so difficult to sit up or walk had disappeared. He easily pushed up on one knee.

Franklin felt his nose. It did not appear to be broken, but plenty of blood had dried on his upper lip and cheek. He attempted to scrape it off, then looked at his fingers. When he saw his hand, he forgot about the blood.

Abruptly, Franklin stood, rolling both hands under his widening eyes. Where were the wrinkles? The varicose veins? The age spots? *Impossible!* Why, these were the very hands that had worked the types on his very first press: strong, nimble—*young!* His fingers went to his cheeks, to his forehead. Where were the creases? The sags? This was a face he hadn't touched in fifty years. One hand jumped to his scalp. There was hair!

It worked!

He cried aloud. "The chamber worked!"

Despite the strange phenomenon that had afflicted him during the process, the oldest fantasy of humankind had still been achieved! The vilest curse which had ever afflicted rich and poor, Catholic and Protestant, master and slave, man and woman—the blight of time, the disease of decay, the curse of *old age*—had been conquered! And old Benjamin Franklin—correction!—*young* Benjamin Franklin, the tamer of lightning, had slain it!

He dropped to the ground again, rolling once in the tall grass. "I am young again!" And then more quietly as he found a clump of wild flowers and buried his face in the petals: "I am *young.*"

In his jubilation, he had been only mildly aware that the fabric of his nightgown had somehow been burned, although the charred edges were long since cold. *Bloodied face, scorched and tattered garments—I must look the part of the devil himself!*

Franklin made a full turn. By degrees his jubilant expression changed to consternation. In daylight he confirmed that this place was a patch of woods. No people were in sight. The location did not much resemble the place he'd seen in those perplexing hallucinations, except for the iron rails that cut through the woods about twenty yards below where he stood. Before yesterday's visions (or had they occurred the day before?) Franklin had never seen such rails. His recollection of the machine that had moved along these rails was vague. It was difficult to separate reality from nightmare.

Fifteen yards above him stretched a road. Just across this road began a field of wheat. To the west flowed a river. The images he had seen were not hallucinations. But if not hallucinations, what were they? A quarter mile in the distance a large house sprang up. Beyond the house were oak and hickory forests, obscuring his view of further dwellings.

Franklin approached the road. At first it had looked like a typical dirt highway. But on closer examination, nothing about this road seemed typical. There were no wheel ruts, no uneven ground—the road ran arrow-straight for what appeared to be several miles. Franklin had thought his job as postmaster had taken him to every corner of New England, yet nothing about this setting seemed remotely familiar.

An object caught the light at the side of the highway; a cylinder of sorts, shiny silver and green. Franklin retrieved it. *Amazing!* The container was comprised of paper-thin metal—so supple it dented under the slightest pressure. Print had been engraved on it in a most clever manner—no ridges or grooves! The colors were splendid, among the brightest, crispest he'd ever seen, and totally unsmudgeable. The container was still a quarter full. He was careful not to spill the remaining fluid as he pronounced the largest words on the can, "Mountain Dew."

Franklin poured a portion of the liquid into his palm. Yellowish, with a sweetish odor. He reread the label to be sure it was, in fact, a beverage and not a lubricant or a poison: *Carbonated water, high fructose corn syrup, sugar, orange juice . . .* Most of the other ingredients were unfamiliar. Some even sounded downright toxic, but he couldn't imagine the fluid to be anything other than a beverage. Delicately, he touched the liquid to his tongue. His face puckered.

Oh, it's awful! So sweet! No wonder someone had tossed it to the side of the highway half consumed. He wiped his palm on the roadside grass.

Atop the can had been engraved the words "Don't litter—Please recycle." Franklin contemplated the meaning of the phrase and wondered why such advice had gone unheeded. Franklin noted that the substance had been manufactured in Somers, New York. He looked around again. Was this New York? How in the devil did he get all the way to New York? And how could New Yorkers have manufactured such a container without his having heard about it? And how—? Heavens! The questions were innumerable!

Franklin heard noise and turned his head. Something approached him, moving up the road—thundering closer and closer. The object traveled faster than any horse-drawn carriage he'd ever known. Its precise shape was blurred by raised dust as well as the vaporous waves of afternoon heat.

The noise it made compared to a stampede of horses, but the object was not drawn by animals, unless the object itself was a kind of animal. It *did* appear to have eyes. A mythological dragon? Franklin recalled an incident in Paris in 1783 when his friend Jacques Charles had launched one of the city's first hot-air balloons—only to have it destroyed forty-five minutes later by the pitchforks of terrified villagers who thought it was a fallen monster. *Oh, French peasants, forgive my petty judgments against your ignorance. Had I a pitchfork, I would undoubtedly stand ready at this moment to deliver a similar assault.*

As the object drew closer, he noticed its wheels. A motorized wagon? A newfangled implement of war? Since he still couldn't be certain that he was in a friendly district, he decided it best to hide himself behind the nearest tree.

He did so hastily and peeked around the trunk. The motor carriage whipped by at a speed that would have defeated the world's fastest horse. All doubt as to whether this was a man-made implement dispelled when Franklin noticed a single passenger inside the coach—a young man facing straight ahead and eating, as best as he could tell, some kind of bread nestled in silverish paper. Within seconds the vehicle was far away.

Fantastic! Franklin regretted having hidden behind the tree. Why hadn't he flagged the driver down? He stepped back into the roadway before the dust settled. *I am* not *in America,* he concluded. *Nor am I in Europe. Somehow I have been transported to part of the globe as yet undiscovered—like Gulliver in Swift's satires.* He was confident that America's distinction as part of a "new world" would soon become obsolete. There was now a world even *newer!*

But perhaps this was not the earth at all, Franklin imagined. Perhaps he was on the moon, or a distant star. Franklin had often listened to the fanatical debates of Christians as they tried to determine the location of the lost ten tribes of Israel. *I may now be the only man alive who could settle this infantile dispute once and for all!*

There was only one way to answer all his questions.

Franklin would have to approach one of this country's denizens and hope that he spoke the same language as indicated on the container of Mountain Dew—or at least some version of French, Italian, or German. He could make himself understood in any of these languages, as well as in Latin. There was another dwelling about a quarter mile down the road. As Franklin set out toward this house, he suddenly felt acutely nervous. Might he be destroyed as a spy or an invader the moment he was discovered? If he could have thought up any other solution to his problem besides a direct confrontation, he'd have gladly pursued it.

He passed a yellow road sign that read, "Discharging of Firearms Prohibited Inside City Limits," followed by an ordinance number. Oddly, the sign was riddled with bullet holes.

As Franklin gazed up into the sky, his heart leapt. Something cut its way across the heavens, leaving a long tail of smoke like a comet, but it was not a comet, nor was it a bird or a balloon. *A machine that can fly?* This was almost too much, even for a mind as supple and inquisitive as Benjamin Franklin's.

He forged on, walking in the grass at the roadside to accommodate his bare feet. His head felt dizzy. Each emotion—trepidation, wonder, loneliness, exhilaration—washed over him successively. Nearing the house, he noticed that the roadway intersected with another road, partially hidden by a line of trees. Several more of these motorized carriages whirred by, only this time they raised no dust. This other road was not of dirt. The shapes and colors of each vehicle varied dramatically, although he noted that four wheels were standard.

As Franklin looked on the house, he was vexed by another flurry of questions. What about those windows? the doors? the fixtures? Extending out from the house was a series of wires which attached to a wooden pole, then reached over to another pole, then another, *ad infinitum.* Franklin was astonished that he could be so unfamiliar with so many of this country's implements and gadgets.

He arrived at the intersection and saw the highway's surface was composed of a kind of asphalt or tar. Franklin marveled at the number of man-hours it must have taken to spread this material. Such an undertaking might have rivaled the pyramids of Egypt.

People in the various motor coaches had seen him now. But the inhabitants of this strange country looked only mildly concerned about his presence. Several drivers stared at him as long as they could before their vehicles passed. Some coaches slowed down, but no one thought it necessary to stop.

Franklin tried to straighten his hair with his fingers, but then he felt silly. The straightest hair in the world could not have drawn attention away from his ridiculous appearance— a burnt and tattered nightgown in broad daylight! The first order of business was to locate some decent clothes.

Before approaching the front door of the house, he peered down the asphalt highway and spotted another sign: *Welcome to Elysia, IL. Home of the Spartans.*

Franklin gasped. *Elysia? Good gracious! It* was *heaven!*

These were the Elysian Fields—the "heaven" of Greek mythology! Mythology? No, indeed! The dead religion of the Greeks was the true religion of the world after all! But according to the sign it was the final resting place only of the Spartans. What about the Athenians? The Romans? The theological implications of this were profoundly confusing. Had he gone to the *wrong* heaven? Franklin squinted and read the

31

numbers at the bottom of the sign: *Pop. 26,540.* Why, this heavenly city wasn't much larger than Philadelphia!

Another coach sped by and its passengers laughingly shouted an obscenity at him with the advice that he put on some clothes. *Obscenity in heaven?* Such seemed out of character. But if obscenity was out of character, what about that gang of ruffians? Perhaps the promise of various ministers throughout his life had come to pass. This was not heaven at all—but *hell!* Franklin had to find some answers before he drove himself mad! But, of course, if this was hell, sending him insane may have been the Adversary's precise intention.

Franklin bounded down the line of tall hedges and toward the open gate. He prayed that someone—anyone— would be home. He hoped desperately that this person would be willing to explain everything. As he was about to enter the yard, Franklin stopped sharply.

There at his feet, disheveled, dusty, slightly crumpled, but still quite readable, lay an item with which Franklin was intimately familiar. Although the size and layout were unusual, the item undoubtedly represented a news periodical.

Franklin gathered the trampled newspaper. His eyes were drawn to its name: *USA Today.* Next, his focus fell on the date of its release: *Tuesday, August 17, 1993.*

Franklin's legs became weak. He staggered into the yard and dropped to his knees. His only cognizance was in the repeated flash of the words, *August 17, 1993.*

This is not my time. Franklin pored over the release date again and again. *1993.*

This is not my world!

The concept of time as a malleable thing had never occurred to Benjamin Franklin, at least not in any practical sense. Of course, every boy and girl ever born had entertained a fantasy of what it might be like to live in the day of the Egyptians, the Romans, the Pilgrims. To walk and talk with Plato, King Arthur, Marco Polo, or Jesus Christ. But to fantasize a visit to a day when every soul the person had ever known would be centuries dead and buried? Such an idea would have been pure lunacy!

How could this have happened? By no conceivable variation had this been Franklin's objective. How foolish to think that he could harness the power of lightning—the power of God! Where might his body have been for two hundred years and forty months? Is this how long it had taken nature to rejuvenate his muscles and cells?

And then it hit Franklin with even greater impact.

They're all dead—Sally, Jane, Richard, Benny, Billy, Polly, Louis, Deborah, Jefferson, Washington, all of them!—dead and buried.

The grief of death was not unknown to Benjamin Franklin, but never had it overwhelmed him so completely. The funeral that should have been his, to be attended by all those who loved him, had suddenly become the funeral of every person who had ever lived in the eighteenth century, to be attended by him alone.

Franklin fell back onto the grass, squeezing his eyes shut and pressing his fists to his temples. "God forgive me," he whispered.

The vanity which had driven him to seek out the fountain of youth was now forcing him to relinquish every custom, mode, and protocol he had ever learned or mastered. As of now, he owned nothing. What's more, he had no means of obtaining anything—not even a meager scrap of food. As pertaining to this day, he *knew* nothing, and he had no idea how he might begin to learn. Not since the morning he arrived at Philadelphia's wharf—a lad of seventeen, a stranger, dirty, fatigued, and only a Dutch dollar and a shilling in copper to his name—had Franklin felt so lost and alone. But even then he had known the basic customs, the general protocol. He'd possessed the skills of a useful trade. And oh! what he wouldn't give now for those filthy work clothes or the equivalent of a Dutch dollar (if, in fact, such means of exchange were even employed in this century!).

Franklin had worked too hard, come too far, to be thrust back into such utter poverty and obscurity. For several minutes, he lay there silently on this stranger's lawn, in this strange day, his body young but his mind disheveled and exhausted.

"Richard Saunders," Franklin mumbled to himself, "what wisdom canst thou provide me now?" None of the maxims of his fictional philomath seemed remotely applicable under the circumstances.

He lay there for several minutes. After a time, the beating of Franklin's heart slowed. He inhaled long and deep, reopened his eyes, and sat up straight.

If there is a way here, it stands to reason, there is a way back. Franklin knew that this logic was fallible—perhaps time was strictly a forward stream—but the thought gave him courage. His stomach growled. Further motivation! Where a sense of loss tempts a man to surrender all, pangs of hunger drive him to go on, at least a little longer.

But where to begin? Franklin glanced again at the newspaper. This seemed as good a place as any to start his twentieth-century familiarization.

For the first time, the implications of the periodical's name struck Benjamin Franklin profoundly: *USA Today*— The United States of America Today! Franklin couldn't help but feel a keen sense of fatherly pride. So the grand experiment had survived for two centuries. Was it still a republic? Had the constitution they had labored so long and hard to design in the summer of '87 endured all this time? It was clear from the paper's boldest headline that at least the nation was still governed by a president. His name was Clinton, and according to the headline he had taken an offensive on a new national health plan. There was some kind of multicolored ink print of him standing in a place called Colorado. Franklin was shocked to see that the portrait recorded an event only three days old. It was not the kind of print carving he was familiar with. The detail and color were particularly fine. The front page featured several more portrait prints—all of them beautifully colored and detailed, as if the picture had been stripped right off the human eye. Was such a thing possible?

Below the Clinton portrait rested a map of Massachusetts and the island of Martha's Vineyard. At last! A place he recognized. The paper expounded upon the president's vacation plans. Frivolous stuff to put in a news periodical, thought Franklin, but it proved that the people of 1993 were just as interested in daily gossip about their leaders as the people of 1790.

In the bottom left corner sat an interesting graph on the incidence of juvenile crime across the nation. The numbers were disturbing. A story at the top of the paper told of the arraignment of two North Carolina teens for the murder of the father of an important person named Jordan. Did the youth of America represent the majority of twentieth-century criminals?

Every sentence printed in the periodical—indeed, every word!—carried volumes of educational subtext. Some of it, however, was impossibly vague. He read the article entitled "AT&T Deal: 'One-stop shopping'" twice and couldn't make heads or tails of any part of it. What in heaven's name was a cellular telephone?

He found a short article at the bottom particularly intriguing and wondered why the publisher had given it so little attention. The headline read "In Presley they trust." The first line went on to say: *Elvis, remembered again Monday on the 16th anniversary of his death, could be the focus of a religion in the making.* Apparently a man named Presley Elvis had been a great "king" in a country called Graceland. His fanatical followers were now worshipping him at his tomb, and many had even reported sightings of his ghost! A fascinating perspective on the founding of a new religion.

Inside, there were articles on the deportation of an Arabian sheik, the pros and cons of gun control, flooding on the Mississippi River, civil war in southeastern Europe, the visit of the Catholic pope to a place called Denver, and the heart-wrenching tale of doctors' efforts to separate a pair of Siamese twins. A thrill leaped in Franklin's soul when he read that the twins were to be treated at the Children's Hospital of Philadelphia, Pennsylvania. Franklin and Dr. Thomas Bond had been instrumental in establishing the very first colonial hospital in Philadelphia in 1755.

More amazement was in store. On page 6A there was a single paragraph of news from every state in the nation. Franklin counted the states with increasing awe. No less than fifty-one! Oh, how the fledgling infant had grown! How it had matured! America appeared to have attained a level of world prominence Franklin could scarcely have thought possible. There among the listed states was Ohio! Once Franklin had sacrificed a small fortune and a lifelong dream on the futile prospect that Ohio could become a colony before he died. And there was Kentucky! And Florida!

There was even a tidbit of news from Pennsylvania. It was on the state's governor—no doubt the latest in a long line of men who had succeeded Benjamin Franklin at that post. Doctors were removing a sliver of muscle tissue from the governor's transplanted heart. Heart and liver transplants? *What a glorious time is this twentieth century!*

When he glanced at the paragraph attributed to Indiana, he couldn't help but notice that a short piece of news had originated from a city called Franklin. Could it be possible . . . ?

There was news from Britain! News from Egypt! News from China! And all of it current—some as recent as yesterday! Even with machines that could fly, how could news travel so fast?

But when Franklin turned another page, his astonishment reached its apex. He found a drawing of the national weather map—a forecast for the entire United States, no doubt more reliable than the lighthearted prognostications of Poor Richard Saunders. For the first time, Franklin took in the total length and breadth of the American nation: a country which ran from ocean to ocean and beyond—from islands in the south seas to a giant mass of territory in the far north.

How far we have come! What a journey it must have been! At last, the fatherly pride that swelled inside Franklin's chest produced a tear on his cheek. And then, in his utter exhaustion, he began to weep, and weep heavily. Not since that day over forty-four years earlier when his four-year-old son Franky had been taken by smallpox had his tears flowed so freely. But his tears today were not solely for his losses. They were equally the product of sweeping, immersing joy. So few men while still in this world had ever lived to see the seeds they'd planted through a lifetime of toil grow into such a magnificent forest. The range of Franklin's emotions caught him up in an ecstasy of self-awareness that few human beings ever experience.

In this ecstasy, Franklin forgot his hunger, he forgot his appearance, and he forgot his dire circumstances. The soft lawn inviting, the sun sinking low into the west, he lay down his head and dropped off to sleep.

CHAPTER 4

"What's he doing now?" Tory inquired, stretching the phone cord as taut as he could without yanking it out of the jack.

Michalene, facing backwards on the couch with her knees on top of the cushions, continued peering out the window. "He just laid down in the grass again. I think he's trying to take a nap."

"On our lawn?" cried Tory.

The brother and sister had been watching the crazy man who had planted himself on their front lawn for twenty minutes now. Dressed as he was in that burnt-out robe, they wondered if he'd just fled the scene of an accident—a car crash or a house fire. They didn't draw their final conclusion that the man was plumb out of his gourd until he started bawling like a baby after reading what must have been a very sad story in the newspaper.

Fifteen-year-old Michalene glanced over at her brother. "What's taking Mom so long?"

"I don't know," Tory answered, the phone still pressed to his ear. "I've been on hold for ten minutes now. Maybe they can't find her. Maybe she's already left. What time was she picking Dad up from the airport?"

"Forget about calling Mom," said Michalene. "I think we should just call the police."

"Nooo way," Tory replied. "I don't want cops anywhere near me—or this house." Although he was only thirteen, Tory had already suffered several minor scrapes with the Elysia Police Department. The incidents hadn't fostered in him much trust for "men-in-blue."

Tory gave up the wait. "I think they forgot about me." He hung up the phone.

"Well, it looks like he's totally zonked now," Michalene observed. "Do you think he's a vagabond?"

"You mean a bum?"

Michalene gave her brother a dirty look. Of *course* that was what she meant. Tory teased her whenever she used a word longer than two syllables. It was getting tiresome.

Tory climbed on the couch beside his sister. "I don't know," he replied. He looked the stranger over one more time. "I still think he came from an accident. Or maybe some kind of weird cult ritual. What idiot would *deliberately* dress up like that? Even bums have standards. I think the accident mixed up his brain."

"Then we should call an ambulance," said Michalene. "He might have a concussion! If he falls asleep his brain could hemorrhage and he could die!"

"If he died on our lawn, could we be sued?" asked Tory.

"How should I know?"

"You're the one who wants to be a lawyer."

"A corporate attorney," Michalene corrected. "Not an ambulance chaser. You dial 911. I'm going to try to wake him up."

"*I* want to wake him up," Tory insisted. He was already headed for the door.

Michalene growled. "You're grounded, remember? If Mom or Dad catch you outside, you'll be executed!"

Tory stepped out into the warm yellow light of the fast-sinking sun. At the moment, he was the man of the house and felt obligated to protect the family and all their material possessions.

The stranger was still fast asleep by the front gate. Tory crept toward him. He walked on the grass instead of the sidewalk to make less noise. *What am I doing?* he thought. Wasn't he supposed to make enough noise to wake the guy up? Still, he remained quiet until he stood directly over the stranger.

The stranger slept on his stomach, using his left arm as a pillow. Tory found it curious: even though his robe was charred and black, there was no evidence of burned or blistered skin. Maybe he was wrong. Maybe a bum *would* deliberately dress like this.

"Hey, you," said Tory.

The man didn't move.

Tory lightly kicked the stranger's leg and spoke a little louder, "Hey, mister!"

Startled, the man leaped to his feet, glaring at Tory as if he were a Martian. Tory yelped and fled toward the house.

"Boy, wait!" the man called.

Tory threw open the front door. Slamming it shut, he called over to his sister on the phone, "Cancel the ambulance! The guy's not hurt!" Tory locked both chain and deadbolt.

"Hold on," Michalene told the 911 operator. "My brother says the man is fine now." Michalene covered the mouthpiece. "What's he doing now?" she asked her brother.

Tory went back over to the window. "Gathering up the newspaper. I think he's going away."

Michalene spoke back into the phone, "Sorry. False alarm. Thanks anyway." She hung up.

"No, wait!" Tory cried. "He's coming toward the house!"

• • •

"I frightened the poor child half to death," Franklin muttered as he approached the door. Certainly his appearance hadn't helped.

The sky was dimming rapidly now. A dog barked in the backyard, alerted by the commotion. Franklin raised his hand and clinked the metal door knocker. As the doorknob turned from inside, he heard the boy crying, "Don't let him in!" followed by a girl chiding, "What's the matter with you? You're *way* too paranoid."

The door opened only a sliver. A small chain went taut and stopped it. The girl's nose pressed into the gap. *A bright, warm face,* thought Franklin. He could tell she was somewhat plump. The boy stood behind his sister. Also an intelligent-looking child. Sandy blond hair, much like his own, and rosy cheeks dotted with freckles. *Odd,* thought Franklin. The lad looked vaguely familiar.

"Can we help you?" asked the girl.

"Yes, you may," said Franklin. "Pardon my appearance. I know it's dreadful. I find myself separated from my store of clothes at the moment. Might I inquire: is the gentleman of the house within?"

"I'm sorry, he's not."

"How about the good woman?" asked Franklin.

"The 'good woman'?"

Franklin suspected he'd misused common vernacular. "Your mama?"

The boy started to giggle. "*Jo mama!*"

They were making sport of him, Franklin realized. Just what *did* they call their mothers in the twentieth century?

"Our mom isn't home either," the girl finally admitted.

"Well, then," said Franklin, "might I inquire as to the names of you two fine children?"

"What business is that of yours?" said the boy.

Franklin drew back his chin. He decided to forgive such discourtesy, reminding himself that this was no longer 1790. Social customs today might be quite different from his century, as different as the customs of England are from India.

"Why, no business at all. I was merely—"

"I think you'd better get off our property," said the boy.

Franklin refused to believe this rudeness was the product of ill breeding. After all, he *was* dressed like a perfect scoundrel. He'd also privileged himself to doze on their lawn. No doubt he would have been equally suspicious of such a loiterer at Franklin Court.

"That might be a wise suggestion," he replied. "But might I be allowed to ask one more question?"

"I'll get rid of him," said the boy. Off he went toward the back of the house.

"What's your question?" asked the girl.

"Is there a place nearby where a man might discover temporary employment or accommodations for a night?"

"The shelter is on the other side of town," said the girl. "Are you new around here?"

Franklin noted that the dog was barking louder than before. "Yes, quite new," said Franklin. "I only just arrived in your fair city yesterday. I have—"

The dog's barking was *much* louder. In fact, the animal was rushing around the side of the house, followed by the boy yelling, "Get 'im, Joker! Kill! Kill!"

In the dim light, Franklin could not see the dog clearly. He could only imagine a mongrel with gums stretched taut, exposing sharp and dripping fangs. Were vicious attack dogs standard fare for twentieth-century households? He did not perceive the golden retriever's panting tongue and wagging tail.

43

Franklin leaped from the porch and dashed toward the wide cement flat on the east side of the house, where a wide escapeway from the yard awaited. A stride or two from the asphalt street, Franklin halted sharply. Around the hedge appeared a long motorized carriage, its eyes ablaze with electrical fire. The carriage veered the blinding, fatal beams onto *him!* Franklin thrust his palms forward in defense. Would it disappear like the machine that had nearly crushed him on the rail?

Mrs. Mickelson slammed on the brakes. The car struck Franklin before it could stop. Franklin's head hit the concrete driveway. He was stretched out cold. Mr. and Mrs. Mickelson jumped out of the car and rushed over to him. Not even Joker's lapping tongue against Franklin's cheek could immediately revive him.

"Oh, my gosh! Oh, my gosh!" cried Mrs. Mickelson.

"I told you someday you were gonna kill somebody if you kept pulling into the driveway like that!" chided Mr. Mickelson.

"Guess I'd better call 911 again," said Michalene. "Gonna need that ambulance after all."

CHAPTER 5

"What's your name?" asked the EMT.

Franklin was unconscious for only four or five minutes. The paramedics arrived as he was coming to. It may have been fortunate that the ambulance had decided to dispatch to the scene based on Michalene's first phone call, even though she'd said it was a false alarm. In a small town like Elysia, paramedics had ample time to investigate *all* alarms, false or true.

Franklin continued to feel groggy. These odd gentlemen who had arrived in the motor carriage topped by a brilliant red flashing light had wrapped his arm in a sort of "squeezing" belt. They also shined a small light into his eyes and helped him hold something cold against the lump on his head.

He answered the EMT as best he could in the confusion. "Name? My . . . Frank—"

"Your first name is Frank? What's your last name, Frank?"

"No. Uh . . . Benjamin."

"Frank Benjamin? Can you tell me what day it is, Mr. Benjamin?"

"Day? August 17th, 1993."

He turned to the other man. "Only a week off," he said,

mildly amused. He turned back to Franklin, more direct. "Try August 24th. What's your address, Mr. Benjamin?"

"My address is . . . 316–318 High Street, Philadelphia, Pennsylvania."

"Hey, I got a sister who lives in Philly," said the EMT. "Her name is Martha. You know 'er?" The other paramedic laughed.

"You're a long way from home, Mr. Benjamin," the EMT continued. "What brings you to Illinois?"

Franklin had nearly regained full coherence, just enough to realize he had a terrible headache. "Is that where I am?"

The only Illinois Franklin knew of was in the region of a river by the same name, far out in the western wilderness. He was at a loss to explain how the chamber could have sent him hundreds of miles westward. Then again, considering the multiple rotations of the earth and its numerous migrations around the sun over the last two hundred and three years, he decided it was fortunate his body hadn't materialized in the middle of an ocean, or in the center of the constellation Orion.

The EMT guessed from "Mr. Benjamin's" statement that he must have jumped off the train without knowing his locality.

"Who burned your clothes?" asked the other paramedic. Since the man's skin wasn't blistered, he assumed the clothing had been torched by another hobo as a vengeful prank while he wasn't wearing them. "And where did you get the nosebleed?"

"A rather unfortunate incident," said Franklin. "Would you gentlemen have a cup of water?"

"I'll get it," said Michalene. She went inside.

"So will he be okay?" asked Mr. Mickelson.

"Yeah, I think so," said the paramedic. "Just a bad bump.

We could take him in for observation, but I'm sure we'd just be dropping him off at the shelter later tonight."

"And what can I expect at this shelter?" asked Franklin.

"They'll give you a bed. Feed you a meal."

Franklin's eyes lit up. "Splendid! I'm absolutely famished."

"How long since you've eaten?" asked Mrs. Mickelson.

"Well, madam, by the growl in my stomach I might venture it's been several hundred years."

The paramedics smiled at Franklin. He was obviously no run-of-the-mill hobo. His style of speech was rather charming.

"He sounds English," Tory observed.

"Oh, no, my dear boy. I can assure you, I am one hundred percent American." Franklin took the cold pack off his head and examined it. *What an interesting pouch,* he thought. *How might they have gotten it so cold in the middle of August?*

"Well, I refuse to put him off on the shelter for dinner," said Mrs. Mickelson. "The least I can do for nearly running him over is to feed him a home-cooked meal."

"You are an angel, madam," said Franklin. "For this I am your most loyal and abject servant."

Gerald Mickelson nudged his wife. "Bonnie, can I talk to you for a second?" He pulled Bonnie out of hearing range. "What do you think you're doing?"

"Practicing what I preach," said Bonnie defensively. "Didn't you read the piece I did two weeks ago on Elysia's homeless? Of course not. You never read *any* of my articles. These people are not untouchables. They're human beings."

"We have no idea who this guy is," said Gerald. "It's obvious he's a first-class con man. Listen to the way he talks."

Franklin had the paramedics and children laughing. When Michalene handed him the water in a brightly painted Disney World commemorative glass with diamond shapes around the rim, Franklin commented that he hadn't drunk from such an elegant chalice since dining with the king of Denmark.

"See what I mean?" said Gerald. "This guy's an *operator.* I'm just waiting for the sudden attack of whiplash and the demand for compensation."

"Gerald, try not to be your usual snobbish self tonight," said Bonnie. "We almost killed a man! We can feed him and take him to the shelter ourselves."

Franklin had developed an interest in the blood-pressure cuff. "What do you call this device?"

"Sphygmomanometer," said the paramedic.

"Gracious! What a marvelous word! What does it say about me?"

"Says you're 120 over 80."

"Is that good?"

"Means you're as healthy as a horse."

"I might have told you as much," said Franklin proudly.

"Do you have a headache?"

"Like a sledgehammer on a harpsichord." Franklin's exuberant tone might have been better suited to the phrase, "Fit as a fiddle."

Further amused, the paramedic handed him some Tylenol. "Take this with the rest of your water." He turned to Mr. and Mrs. Mickelson while his partner packed up the gear. "He's fine. I'll leave him with you if you want. Just keep an eye on him for a few hours. If he complains of dizziness or starts vomiting or convulsing or something, give us a call, but I don't think there'll be any problems."

"You gentlemen have been most affable. I am in your debt."

"Don't mention it. You just take care of yourself, Frank."

"With the help of these fine people, that I will do."

There's the first hint, thought Gerald. *He's gonna want much more than dinner.*

Bonnie stepped forward to introduce herself. "I'm Bonnie Mickelson. This is Gerald and our two children, Torrence and Michalene."

"What did you say your last name was?" asked Franklin.

"Mickelson," Bonnie repeated.

Franklin had heard that name before. No, he hadn't *heard* it—he had *read* it.

"Are you a relation to the Mickelson who is running for president to replace Mr. Clinton?" Franklin wondered.

Gerald laughed. "I think you got the wrong Mickelson."

How strange, thought Franklin. What exactly had he seen in that peculiar vision of the political rally? The images pulsed in his mind with all the clarity of his most striking memories.

"So, what *did* happen to your clothes?" asked Tory.

Franklin's headache throbbed relentlessly. "That is a wonderfully long story," he said, pressing a temple. "Better I should tell it later."

"Let's get you inside," said Bonnie. "Gerald, do you have something Mr. Benjamin could change into?"

Gerald nodded halfheartedly.

Franklin suspected the *nom de plume* he had fallen into of "Frank Benjamin" might be prudently adopted for the time being. He also determined to curb his numerous questions. No doubt all these twentieth-century contrivances were taken for granted by these modern Americans. Too many questions might make him appear all the more out of

49

his element. However, as Michalene flipped on the wall switch and instantly illuminated the front room with brilliant light, Franklin felt sorely tempted to break his resolution. What a remarkable, *remarkable* thing!

And then there was the box in the sitting room! It was all he could do to walk past the living, moving image without stopping slack-jawed to gape. What was the image? An eagle? Yes! The swooping image of an eagle had somehow projected itself inside a wooden box in the family sitting room!

Gerald wasn't exactly Franklin's size. The philosopher was built like a wrestler while Gerald was thin and tall. Gerald located an old pair of sweat pants and a T-shirt with a slogan that read: *No one else cares, but my dog still loves me.* Gerald rarely wore them, especially the T-shirt, since the slogan seemed not so humorous as depressing these days. Over the last several months its sentiment had hit a little too close to home.

Franklin also found the slogan rather dreary, but he graciously accepted the clothing. The golden retriever on the T-shirt appeared considerably more docile than the slavering mongrel that had earlier attempted to take a bite out of his backside.

Adding a pair of Fruit of the Loom briefs to the stack, Gerald said, "You can change in the bathroom."

"You are most kind," said Franklin.

Before Franklin had shut the door, Gerald couldn't prevent himself from saying, "Please, uh . . . don't take anything."

"I would not consider it, sir."

Gerald nodded, slightly embarrassed. But the statement had to be said.

Alone inside the bathroom, Franklin allowed himself a

moment's pause. He shuddered gleefully. With his fists raised and clenched, he had all the appearance of an orphan in the palace of a king. Why, even *more* wonders surrounded him. What was this? An indoor outhouse? An automatic wash basin? It was all so spectacular and beautiful! But nothing could have struck him more deeply than the beauty of the reflection looking back at him in the mirror.

As Franklin edged closer, his eyes again filled with tears. At last he had seen the full miracle of the chamber. He knew that face. He was thirty years of age again. Perhaps thirty-two. A torrent of memories and sentiments rushed back. He remembered thinking he was so *old* back then. So wise. If only he had known. Franklin touched his fingers to both cheeks. The tears had clouded his vision now. He pinched them off by closing his eyes. When he opened them, he saw the cornea had reddened and the tears had carved a trail down his cheeks, but the reflection was no less beautiful.

Franklin turned the faucet knobs and—sure enough— water pumped out. *Hot* water no less! He took a wash cloth and washed his face. Beside the sink he found a bowl with bands of assorted colors. The bands were stretchable! An elastic band! This may have been the most profound invention he'd yet observed. Franklin took the brush and combed back his hair. Then he used the rubber band to make a pony-tail. It had been decades since he'd worn his hair like this. (It had been decades since he'd had enough hair to do so!)

Discovering the flusher on the toilet, he couldn't help but watch what happened when he pushed it down. He then noticed an outlet beside the mirror into which several gadgets had been plugged by way of a long cord.

Could it be? Franklin touched the two holes with his finger. If those holes accessed the kind of power he suspected, it would explain everything. He poked around and found a bobby pin. Pinching the tiny metal instrument between two fingers, he floated it toward one of the holes in the bottom outlet. Gingerly, he poked the end inside.

The jolt threw Franklin back. He kept his footing, but in the process he knocked the shaving cream and the hair spray onto the floor.

Gerald's voice called through the door, "Are you all right in there?"

Franklin shook himself. "Perfectly all right."

It *was* electricity! The twentieth century had effectively harnessed what in his day had been little more than a philosophical amusement. Never had Franklin quite conceived that his little experiments could lead to such a worldwide transformation. He had been impressed enough when his electricity had roasted a turkey. If only he had known that someday this power would enrich, in the most practical and basic ways, the lives of every human being on the planet!

We were little more than savages! Franklin concluded. How could the citizens of this day restrain from leaping for joy every moment of their lives? Once more, he sighed happily at his image in the mirror. Then he removed his charred nightgown and climbed into his fresh, twentieth-century clothes.

· · ·

As Franklin emerged, Gerald was sitting on the bed. The father of the house wasn't quite ready to leave this hobo unsupervised.

Gerald held his oldest pair of sneakers. "Here. You might as well have these too."

"Oh, my. Again, and with all sincerity, I thank you." Franklin slipped them over his stockingless feet. The shoes were well worn and a half size too big. He didn't mind. The design was so intriguing!

"Do I look agreeable?"

"You look great, Frank," said Gerald tiredly.

"I am most impressed by these undergarments," added Franklin. "Marvelously comfortable."

Gerald smiled. "Glad you like 'em." He arose. "I think my wife has cooked up something in the kitchen."

"Splendid. Where might I deposit these rags?" He indicated the charred nightgown.

Gerald took them daintily. "I'll deposit them in the garbage, if you don't mind."

"I cannot imagine a better place."

In the hallway, Franklin paused at one of the photographs on the wall. "You have so many portraits. Are these kind very expensive?"

"Depends on the photographer, I s'pose."

Franklin noted *three* children in the picture. "I see that you have one more arrow in your quiver." He was confident the surest way to a man's heart was to take an interest in his family. Gerald, however, acted reluctant. Franklin got the impression that Gerald hadn't looked at this picture for a very long time.

"Yes," said Gerald. "That's about five years ago."

"And who is this charming little girl?"

"That's Carolyn. She, uh . . . she died. Drowned. Three summers ago."

Gerald said it with such matter-of-factness. Franklin had to look behind his eyes to see the pain. He knew that pain. It had been over fifty years since he'd buried his own four-year-old son. Yet he remembered the pain as if it were yesterday. Franklin considered expounding the details of Franky's death. He thought better of it. Another moment, perhaps. To a man in such pain, only the proper timing can convince him that others have equally sorrowed.

"I'm dreadfully sorry," said Franklin.

Gerald's eyes lingered a bit. He nodded once to close the subject. "Well, let's eat. I'm sure you'll want to get to the shelter early to get a good night's sleep."

"On the contrary," said Franklin. "I feel more awake and alive than I have in years—*no!*—decades!"

For dinner Bonnie served up the leftover fried chicken and corn from Sunday. She also prepared instant mashed potatoes, fresh from the microwave. Franklin marveled at all the appliances in the kitchen, aching to know the function of each and every one. He was surprised to see only two plates on the dining room table.

"Are we to eat alone?" Franklin inquired.

"I'll eat later," said Michalene.

"I already ate," said Tory.

"I never eat after seven," said Bonnie.

Gracious, how the world had changed! Food preparation had apparently become so convenient, a meal was no longer a family event. The two children decided to join them at the table anyway, more to gape than anything else. The boy, Torrence, looked amused as Franklin carefully unfolded his napkin and placed it in his lap. Such manners from a hobo seemed out of character.

Bonnie stood in the kitchen, holding open the refrigerator door. "What would you like to drink? We have Diet Coke, orange juice, skim milk, Mountain Dew . . . "

"Not Mountain Dew," said Franklin. "Did you say orange juice? That would be delightful!" A cabinet for cold storage! Had snow cellars become obsolete? Was there any luxury that this generation lacked?

"So, Mr. Benjamin," said Bonnie, filling his glass, "have you been on the road long?"

Franklin was so pleasantly engrossed in devouring his chicken leg that he didn't hear the question. "Pardon me?"

"How long ago did you leave Philadelphia?"

"Oh, not long at all. Not more than a few days."

"Are you traveling across the country?" asked Michalene.

"I hadn't considered it, young lady. That sounds like a wonderful idea. Does it take long to make such a trip?"

"Depends on how you go, I guess."

"And what means are the swiftest?"

"Airplane, of course."

"Airplane! Yes! I saw one earlier in the day."

Franklin gathered from the raised eyebrows and quirked expressions that he was revealing far too much of his ignorance. He wanted to ask how swiftly an airplane traveled, but he bit his tongue.

"I guess this is the first time you've been to Elysia?" said Gerald.

"Yes, it is. To be perfectly honest, until this day I had not set foot farther west than Fort Gnadenhutten on the Indian frontier." Franklin feared he'd stuck his foot in it again. "Have you . . . heard of Fort Gnadenhutten?"

The family shook their heads. Franklin guessed the fort must be called something else by now, if indeed it still stood at all. "But you have heard of Indians, am I right?"

Again the confused expressions.

"Are you from Jupiter or something?" asked Tory.

Franklin wondered if it might be best to keep his mouth stuffed with mashed potatoes. Was it futile to think he could carry on a normal conversation in this century? Perhaps he should just tell them the truth—that he was a visitor from the eighteenth century and needed to be educated on modern vernacular and convention. Surely he wasn't the *first* such visitor . . . was he?

With all the ingenious inventions he had witnessed thus far, it seemed inconceivable that *someone* out there had not duplicated his chamber. Any moment he expected some member of the family—perhaps this inquisitive little girl—to burst out with the conclusion: "Oh, now I get it! He's just one of those time-traveler persons who visit our century from time to time. So what century are *you* from?"

The absence of such a proclamation left Franklin fearfully suspicious that his chamber had *not* been duplicated. What might be in store for him if they realized his origins? Might they burn him at the stake like a Salem witch? He simply *had* to be more careful of his words!

"I take it," said Franklin, "that you do not entertain many people such as myself?"

Bonnie, of course, interpreted his question as referring to homeless people, not time travelers.

"Unfortunately, no," said Bonnie. "But I'm determined to change that. I'm a firm believer that the homeless should not be wards of the state. If everyday citizens like us continually refuse to lend a hand and shoulder the burden on a personal, intimate level, I don't believe the problem will ever be solved."

Gerald squirmed in his seat. Mr. Benjamin might easily interpret his wife's harangue as an invitation to hound them for money.

Franklin found Bonnie's views on this apparently widespread twentieth-century problem stimulating. As well, he felt this might be a good opportunity to discuss a matter on a philosophical level without introducing anachronisms.

"I quite agree with this view, Mrs. Mickelson, keeping

in mind that such personal, intimate involvement would be better focused if it provided the poor and the idle with opportunities to be industrious and self-sufficient."

Gerald did a double take. Such detached philosophies from a hobo were astonishing.

"How refreshing to hear," said Bonnie, "especially from someone in your, well . . . circumstances."

Franklin was on a roll. "To part with the bounty of one's purse too frequently and demand nothing in return—not even gratitude—will in time irreparably damage the spirit and esteem of the most noble beggar. 'Tis much easier for us to part with a guinea, much harder to part with a gift of our time and talents. Yet if you teach a poor man to shave himself and keep his razor in order, you may contribute more to the happiness of his life than in giving him a *thousand* guineas."

Franklin had turned his attention back to his chicken leg, so he did not immediately notice the expressions of shock all around the table. It was almost as if Mr. Benjamin did not consider himself a part of the homeless community.

"You mean a thousand guinea *pigs?*" asked Tory.

Franklin thought a moment. "Coins? Currency?"

"How come you talk so different?" Tory demanded.

"Do I talk different?" asked Franklin.

"Yeah, like Shakespeare or something?"

"Perhaps I am too much a student of antiquity," Franklin replied. "I fear it may have influenced my speech."

"Can't you talk normal?"

"Tory!" scolded his mother.

"I like the way he talks," said Michalene. "I could sit here and listen to him for hours."

Gerald noticed that Franklin had pretty well cleaned his

plate. "I think we should get going. I'll drive you to the shelter."

"No need to rush him," said Bonnie.

"It's perfectly all right, madam," said Franklin cheerfully. "I have infringed upon your hospitality long enough."

Gerald opened up his billfold and pulled out a one hundred dollar bill. "If you can, don't think of this as charity. Think of it as compensation for that bump on your head."

"Don't be absurd," said Franklin. "You were not to blame. I was equally at fault. I would feel much more compensated if you advised me as to where I might find employment."

Bonnie faced her husband. "Haven't you heard what he's been saying, Gerald? He doesn't want a handout. He wants an opportunity."

Gerald had thought Franklin's speech was mostly bunk and that the hobo's tune would change the moment he caught sight of a one hundred dollar bill.

"So what do you want me to do, Bonnie? Bring him on as my newest managing director?"

"Isn't there something he can do around here tomorrow?" She turned to Franklin. "Would you be willing to do some yard work? With my new job at the *Gazette* and with all the classes I'm taking at the college, things have gotten pretty out of hand this summer."

"I would be delighted!" said Franklin.

Gerald sighed in great exasperation. What was his wife trying to prove? She knew full well that tomorrow he had to work all day in his office. Even though Gerald's office was in his den at the back of the house, this man—this stranger!—would be totally unsupervised for most of the day. He couldn't help but wonder if Bonnie was deliberately trying to add stress to his life. She may have felt she had just cause. During the drive home Gerald had confessed to her a fact which both of them had known for years: that their marriage was hopelessly on the rocks. Weren't their lives complicated enough without adding charity work for the homeless? The only way he could think to snap Bonnie to her senses was to suggest something outrageous.

"I've got it!" said Gerald sarcastically. "Why should we take him to the shelter at all? He can just sleep here for the night! He can sleep in the living room with all the silver and china cabinets—he can sleep directly across from the children's bedrooms. Wouldn't that be a good idea, honey?"

"I think that's a wonderful idea!" said Bonnie.

Gerald's face flushed. How could his suggestion have backfired? Didn't she comprehend the risk? He had forgotten how insanely naive Bonnie could be in her trust of the human race.

Franklin, however, caught the sarcasm. "Perhaps this shelter would be better suited to my needs."

"Nonsense," said Bonnie. "You can sleep on the couch."

Gerald's eyes thinned. Now he understood his wife's motives. With this hobo taking up the couch, he would be forced to sleep on the considerably smaller, considerably less comfortable couch in his den. Oh, she could be a conniving woman.

Gerald pulled out a second hundred dollar bill and held them both toward Franklin. "This is your last chance, Frank. Two hundred dollars. Otherwise tomorrow you'll be working for minimum wage."

"I will take only what I earn," said Franklin, glancing down at the bills. "I was rather looking forward to a hard day's—"

The sentence caught in Franklin's throat. His eyes glued

to the one hundred dollar bill. His next sentence came out uneasily.

"Might I . . . I must . . . Please—would you allow me to examine that currency? I assure you I will return it."

Gerald hesitated. He examined the bills first himself, wondering if Mr. Benjamin had spotted some kind of counterfeiting technique or something. Reluctantly, he handed the bills over.

It's me! Franklin realized. There he was, the balding diplomat, the venerable Doctor Franklin, wearing that same fur-collar coat which had become so famous to his friends in France. He felt certain the image had been taken from one of the Duplessis portraits, just one of several dozen paintings he'd posed for during his decade at Passy as the American ambassador. Duplicates of such portraits had been distributed throughout Europe, adorning everything from snuff boxes to pocket knives to fine porcelain. *And now, over two centuries later, the currency of the United States!*

How could this upstanding twentieth-century family have understood the pride which leaped in Franklin's breast as he gazed at that one hundred dollar bill. His image on the national currency could mean only one thing—the name of Benjamin Franklin had not been forgotten. Did they consider him a father of their country? The family all looked at one another again with cockeyed expressions and shrugging shoulders. Franklin even caught the little boy shaking his head and uttering the words, "Total weirdo." Franklin continued to gaze at the wrinkled green currency.

"It's beautiful," he said absently. "I am beside myself."

"Like I said, if you want it, it's yours," said Gerald uneasily.

Franklin gave back the money. "Tomorrow I will earn it honestly."

"Nope, sorry," said Gerald. "At minimum wage it will take you at least *two* days to earn it."

"Maybe three," said Bonnie. "And I'm sure we can keep you busy at *least* that long." Then, turning to Gerald: "Can't we, dear?"

Gerald was growing rather tired of the taste of his own foot.

• • •

Franklin was able to convince Mr. and Mrs. Mickelson that his odd behavior was the result of exceptional fatigue. Such a confession only did more to firm Bonnie's resolve that tonight he would sleep in their living room rather than at the shelter. Secretly, she planned to let him sleep on the couch for two or three days, forcing Gerald to sleep in the den with that computer and fax machine he loved so much. There *was* a part of her that enjoyed seeing her husband squirm. Gerald's plan, as outlined in the car that evening, was to announce their impending divorce to the children in four days—on Saturday night. Gerald had resolved to move out on the first of September. Bonnie had no intention of making things easier for him until then.

Gerald could do or say nothing as Bonnie began laying out blankets on the couch for Mr. Benjamin. After all, it had all been his suggestion. He locked the china and silver cabinet and dragged his den sofa over by the door so he could see out into the living room and keep an eye on their guest. Gerald considered himself a light sleeper. He felt certain he would rouse at the slightest movement. Yet when his daughter, Michalene, crept out of her room at 3:00 A.M., her father's snores were uninterrupted.

Michalene had originally awakened at 2:00 A.M. She lay awake for an hour pondering the strange guest who was sleeping in the front room. Something wasn't right about this man. She was convinced of it. The way he talked. The things he said. It was as if he didn't belong here. Mr. Benjamin was like a fish out of water, like Tarzan in downtown Chicago. Something deep inside her, perhaps an instinct known only to fifteen-year-old girls, convinced her that things just didn't fit. She was determined to figure out why.

The only progress she thought she could make toward solving this mystery at 3:00 A.M. was to wander into the living room and have another look at Frank Benjamin's face. The TV still glowed, the volume was low. An old western with Kirk Douglas and Burt Lancaster played on cable. Mr. Benjamin had apparently watched television until he dropped off. Michalene noted that two volumes of the *Encyclopaedia Britannica* were missing from the shelf beside the television. One of the volumes sat on the carpet. The other lay on the couch. Mr. Benjamin had fallen asleep with his hand sandwiched inside the pages. Michalene edged closer. She was determined to learn what subjects Frank Benjamin had found so interesting in the *Encyclopaedia Britannica.*

The volume on the floor had been opened and turned upside down, so as not to lose the place. It was Macropaedia, volume 28. Michalene knelt down and turned it over. In the dim light of the television screen she perceived that he had been reading page 663. The article was on "Time." *Time?* How odd that someone would randomly pick up an encyclopedia and look up the subject of "Time." She turned it over again.

Carefully, she slipped the second volume out from under Mr. Benjamin's hand, inserting her thumb where he had been reading. This was Macropaedia, volume 19, page 559. The article was on Frederick the Great. Michalene crinkled her nose. *Frederick the Great?* Was that what Mr. Benjamin had been reading about? Not quite. The article on Frederick the Great was just beginning. Another article had ended on the left side of the page. She looked for the heading. And what was the subject of the preceding article?

Benjamin Franklin.

CHAPTER 6

Two hours before he fell asleep, it finally occurred to Franklin where he had seen the boy. The moment of recognition came when Tory crept into the kitchen for a late-night glass of milk. The lad decided that rather than trouble himself to find a cup, he'd simply drink out of the container. When he noticed Franklin watching him, he became startled and spilled milk down his chin.

"Oh, it's only you," said Tory. "I thought it was Mom. She doesn't like me to put my mouth on the top. She thinks I'll give everybody diphtheria."

Franklin did not reply. He was too shaken. The reaction on the boy's face had triggered his memory.

It's him! Franklin cried inwardly. *This is the boy I saw fall from the pipe! The very lad who drowned in the river!*

And yet how could this be? The boy stood before Franklin now, perfectly alive and healthy. It made no sense!

"Well, good night," said the boy, uncomfortable with the expression on Franklin's face.

"Yes," Franklin replied obliviously. "Good night."

But as Tory attempted to walk past him, Franklin caused him to stop. "My boy, did you . . . suffer a frightening accident of late? A fall into a river? Two days ago perhaps?"

"Fall in a river? I've never fallen in no river. You're thinkin' of my sister, Carolyn. She's the one who drowned."

Franklin concentrated hard. *No.* It was not a girl he had seen fall from the pipe. It was a boy. *This* boy.

"My apologies," said Franklin. "Good night."

"Yeah," said Tory uneasily. "You better get some sleep, Mr. Benjamin."

"Perhaps you're right."

Franklin settled down on the couch. How strange it was to have been rescued from another night in the streets and possible starvation by *this* particular family. A family whose son he had seen fall into the river. A family named Mickelson!—the same name as the candidate he had seen running for the office of President of the United States.

The perplexity of it all gave Franklin unexpected insomnia. Before falling asleep he looked up the subject of Time in the bookshelf encyclopedia hoping to discover some clues about what might have happened to him, particularly during those brief interstices when the landscapes and colors spun back and forth.

The encyclopedia volumes were an amazing resource. Never had Franklin seen such a wealth of knowledge collected into a single set of books. But in spite of all the new information on time—rhythms and dynamics and relativistic effects (including some theories that utterly shattered those of Sir Isaac Newton!)—he realized that time still remained one of the universe's most profound conundrums.

Franklin wondered if he might find an account of his own life in the encyclopedia. More importantly, might he find an account of Benjamin Franklin's death? He was surprised to read in the final paragraph a description not only of Franklin's death on April 17, 1790, but also an account of his funeral, described as the "most impressive funeral" that Philadelphia "had ever seen."

But I never died! protested Franklin. *How could they have held a funeral without a corpse?*

Franklin needed more information than this brief article provided. He wanted to read an exact description of the circumstances surrounding his death and funeral, if any such account existed. But how could it, since it was 1993 and he was still alive? The encyclopedia listed an extensive bibliography. There appeared to be at least ten respectable biographies of Benjamin Franklin's life. Certainly one of these went so far as to mention that Franklin's body had mysteriously disappeared on April 17, 1790, and that a funeral was held despite a missing corpse.

Franklin decided, as he dropped off to sleep, that before he could draw any firm conclusions about what had happened to him or about the strange events he had witnessed as the world was spinning, he had to obtain one or perhaps all of these biographies.

• • •

In the morning Franklin's joints had stiffened. He thought nothing of it. After all, his body had undergone a rather substantial transformation within the last forty-eight hours. He worked the stiffness out by pacing the living room. In a few minutes he felt considerably better. He opened a window and inhaled the morning air. He regretted that he had not been given a private room. That way he might have shed all his clothes and basked in the buff, as had been his waking routine for most of his life.

At breakfast, Franklin discovered that he did not like Captain Crunch, nor did he much care for Cocoa Puffs. He did, however, become an instant fan of Post Raisin Bran, recalling fondly his boyhood when he had sacrificed food to purchase books, often subsisting on little more than a handful of raisins.

Michalene grilled him with questions. "How old are you, Mr. Benjamin?"

"I would approximate my age at thirty-two."

"You mean you don't know exactly?"

It *was* an odd way to answer. "Thirty-two," he confirmed.

"Where were you born?" asked Michalene.

"Boston, Massachusetts," Franklin replied.

"How many brothers and sisters do you have?"

"Well, now, that would depend," said Franklin. "My father was twice married. By his first wife there were seven children. When she died, he married my mother, and by her there were ten more, of which I was the youngest son."

Tory's eyes bugged out. "Seventeen kids? How did anybody ever use the bathroom?"

"We were forced to impose a lottery. Only the winner used such facilities on a given day." Franklin winked.

"Please!" Michalene glared at her brother. *"I'm* asking the questions." She turned back to Franklin. "How come last night you said you were from Philadelphia?"

"That is where I journeyed as a lad of seventeen to make my fortune."

"You mean you ran away from home?"

"Actually, from my brother James. I was his printer's apprentice."

"His what?" asked Tory.

"His personal slave, in a manner of speaking," Franklin clarified.

"Wow!" said Tory. "I wish I had a little brother for a slave."

"I'm certain he would have liked it no more than I."

Michalene continued. "So what happened? What kept you from making your fortune?"

"I'm convinced I *did* make my fortune, dear child."

"So when did you become a homeless bum?" asked Tory.

Michalene scowled. "Ignore my little brother," she told Franklin. "The way he's going, it shouldn't be much longer before he's shipped off to reform school."

Tory's face reddened. He wasn't sure why he didn't want Mr. Benjamin to know about his recent exploits of shoplifting and vandalism. Tory often bragged about such things to his parents' friends just to make his parents uncomfortable. He would never admit it out loud, but he sort of liked Frank Benjamin. Maybe that's why he had to be rude. Then it wouldn't be so bad when, like nearly everyone else, Frank disappointed him.

Franklin did not give Michalene a chance to explain her statement. He put his arm around Tory's shoulder and said, "On the contrary, Torrence's query is an intelligent one. To answer it I must advise you both not to judge circumstances by what they seem. Perhaps I have left my fortune behind to embark upon a grand adventure exploring the great wide world."

"Yeah, right," said Tory. "Then what brought you to 'Dudsville, USA?'"

"Remember, Torrence," said Franklin, "memories are the sum of who we are. The place where you were born will always command a portion of you."

"Then those are memories I'd prefer to forget," said Tory. "And stop calling me Torrence. Only my dad calls me Torrence. When he's mad."

"What name would you prefer?" Franklin inquired.

"Tory."

"Is that your name or your political persuasion?" said Franklin.

Bonnie Mickelson entered the kitchen. She overheard Franklin and laughed. Her children looked at her strangely. She explained Franklin's joke. "Tory is another name for a British loyalist. Two days ago I don't think I would have gotten your joke either, Mr. Benjamin. We've begun studying the Revolution in American Heritage."

"You don't say!" said Franklin. "Is this American Heritage a kind of philosophical society?"

"It's a class. I'm taking a few courses at our local junior college on Tuesdays and Thursdays. It's all part of the same degree I've been working on for the past fifteen years. I just keep plugging away."

"Little strokes fell great oaks, madam," said Franklin. "You should be commended for your tenacity."

"Thank you for saying so," said Bonnie. "My husband has always thought it was a waste of time."

"Might I be allowed to attend one of these lectures?" Franklin requested.

Bonnie's face shined approval. She was still playing the good Samaritan to a homeless vagrant. "Why, I'd be delighted to help you on the road to improving yourself, Mr. Benjamin. The class is large enough that I'm sure no one would mind if you went one time. Maybe if you applied for assistance from the state, they would help you to enroll."

"I would also be interested to know if there is a subscription library nearby," said Franklin.

"The largest library in town is right on campus," Bonnie confirmed.

Franklin was amazed. "Your city has more than one library?"

"Two actually. There's the county library on Adams, but

it's much smaller. You'll enjoy the one on campus a lot more. Tomorrow we'll make a day of it." She looked at her watch. "I'd better get off to work."

As soon as she stepped out the door, Gerald entered the kitchen. He appeared to have been waiting for his wife to leave.

"Okay, Frank," said Gerald. "I'll get you started. If you don't mind, I'd prefer it if you stayed outside until my wife gets home."

"I understand," said Franklin. He downed his last spoonful of cereal. "Let us get cracking, shall we?"

Gerald turned to his son. "I expect you to help Mr. Benjamin later. You're still grounded till tomorrow, you know."

"I know," said Tory brazenly. "Don't worry. After school starts next week, I'll be out of your hair for another nine months."

Gerald sighed. He decided not to respond to his son's sarcasm. After all, in a few days his children might, in certain fundamental ways, be out of his life much longer than nine months. Gerald refused to think about it. He led Franklin toward the front door.

After her father and Mr. Benjamin were gone, Michalene growled in exasperation. "I had a lot more questions I wanted to ask him."

"Why all the questions?" Tory wondered.

"Don't you think there's something a little bizarre about Mr. Frank Benjamin?"

"Yeah," said Tory. "He's a bit crazy. So what?"

"It's almost as if he doesn't belong here."

"Belong where?"

"Anywhere!"

"I don't get it."

"It's not just that he talks funny. He doesn't seem to *know* anything. *Basic* things. Like knowing that an airplane is the fastest way to get across the country."

"Technically," said Tory. "The space shuttle would be faster. Or a satellite."

"Don't be an idiot. What I'm saying is that I think Mr. Benjamin is hiding something."

Tory taunted his sister. "I think you're onto something, Sis. Frank Benjamin is an alien life-form. His superiors sent him ahead as a scout just before they blow up the earth. That would mean Mr. Benjamin's face is merely a clever disguise. Underneath he's this hideous, maggot-looking monster!" Tory let out a scream.

"Shut up, doughhead. I'm totally serious."

"So what do you think he's hiding?" asked Tory.

Michalene shook her head. "All I know is, there's something really weird going on. I'm gonna find out what it is."

· · ·

Do more than is required.

Do it faster than anticipated.

Do it better than expected.

These had always been Franklin's mottoes as a young man in the employ of others. He felt certain that such ideals had contributed greatly to his early success and independence. He hoped that as he continued his application of such attitudes he would earn Mr. Mickelson's trust. It soon became clear, however, as Gerald dispassionately announced his list of chores, that it didn't much matter to him whether Franklin did the jobs or not.

"You could mow the lawn, I guess. If you want, you could trim the hedges. It's so late in the summer, none of this

71

really matters anymore. The lawnmower's in the shed around back."

Gerald's pride of ownership appeared to have dwindled.

"And if I need instructions on how to operate this device—this lawnmower—might I inquire of your son?" asked Franklin.

"Yeah. Ask Tory everything," Gerald confirmed. "I've got a full slate today. Sunday afternoon I'm flying to Dallas. I'm presenting an offer on a shopping mall first thing Monday morning."

"So is this your vocation? To buy and sell property?"

"Part of it. I manage a commercial real estate portfolio for a firm out of Chicago."

"How interesting," said Franklin. "I would be fascinated to learn how such business is transacted in the twentieth"— he caught himself—"these days."

"Are you familiar with this business, Frank?"

"Oh, I doubt very much my experience compares with yours. But I once owned property and rights in Philadelphia, Boston, Ohio, Georgia, and Nova Scotia, among other places."

"Really? So what happened, Frank? How come—?"

Gerald realized the answer was probably more compli-cated than he wished to get into at the moment. He was also conscious of the possibility that Mr. Benjamin was a patho-logical liar.

"Never mind," said Gerald. "If I can pull off this one deal, it'll double my income this year."

"How exciting," said Franklin. "What are your plans for this newly acquired wealth?"

"Oh, I've always got plans," said Gerald, almost defen-sively, as if it was a question often repeated by his wife. "Reinvest mostly. Seems like you never quite have enough, know what I mean?" Gerald winked and turned to go back inside. As an afterthought, he pulled out a twenty-dollar bill. "Oh, and here. A small advance. If Bonnie wants you working around the house a few days, you might want to get some other clothes. There's a secondhand store a few blocks down on Chestnut Street."

"You have been incredibly gracious," said Franklin sincerely.

Franklin walked around to the shed. As soon as he stepped inside, he realized it was hopeless to imagine he could operate this so-called lawnmower without instruction. He wasn't even certain which implement it was. One device he examined read "snow blower." That couldn't be it. Even after Franklin found the item which most likely fit the purpose, he didn't have the slightest idea how to make it run. He knocked on the door and requested Tory's assistance.

As Tory followed Franklin into the shed, he glanced back at the house. His sister was watching them through her bedroom window.

Inside the shed, Tory put his arms on his hips and asked accusingly, "How come you don't know how to start a lawnmower?"

"I never had occasion to use one," said Franklin, "although I certainly would have enjoyed it."

"There's a *lot* of stuff you don't seem to know," said Tory. "My sister thinks you're hiding something from us."

Franklin laughed. "Your sister is sharp as a tack. Every man has secrets, my young friend. Some he should be allowed to retain to his grave, don't you think? Are there not secrets bottled inside of you?"

"Sure," said Tory. "I'll tell you mine if you tell me yours."

"That may indeed, in due time, become an amicable trade-off," said Franklin.

"I'll even tell you my secrets first," said Tory. "Did you know my parents hate each other? It's absolutely true. Now tell me one of your secrets."

"Ah, now that isn't quite fair," said Franklin. "A secret not about oneself is little more than gossip."

"Wanna know another secret?"

"Well, not if—"

"They're getting divorced. They haven't told us yet. I kinda think they're waiting for the right moment. Timing is everything to Mom. *Now* it's your turn."

"Unfortunately," said Franklin, "that's not quite what I had in mind either."

"Okay, I got it," said Tory. "Once I put some of Joker's droppings in a paper bag and lit it on fire in front of Chip Gillespie's door. Chip came out and stomped on it. He never found out who it was, but"—Tory bounced his thumb on his chest proudly—"it was me."

"Ah, now that's a *proper* secret," said Franklin. Then, in a tone oddly serious, he added, "You are a clever boy, Tory. A bit misdirected in your cleverness, perhaps. But exceedingly clever nonetheless."

The boy looked uncomfortable with such compliments. "So do I get to hear one of your secrets or not?"

Franklin smiled. "All in good time, my clever friend."

Tory sighed in exasperation. "Well, try to tell me before I'm forty, okay? I might not live that long."

Franklin's face became gravely concerned. "You mustn't say such things, young man. I assure you, you shall live to be much older than forty."

Tory was surprised by Franklin's vexation. "Don't have a cow. It was just a joke."

Tory started the mower and gave Franklin brief instructions on how to empty the lawn bag when it was full.

As Franklin started down the first edge of the backyard, his uneasiness over the boy's statement did not dispel. He was ready to conclude that he had glimpsed a brief moment in this boy's ill-fated future. Was it inevitable that Tory should die? Was the boy correct in assessing that he might never live to see his fortieth or even his *fourteenth* birthday? The thought coiled in the pit of Franklin's stomach.

When Tory was forty years old, the year would be two thousand twenty. *Strange,* thought Franklin. He recalled seeing that number somewhere recently. Franklin's mind flashed back to his short-lived vision of the political rally. He strained to recollect the exact wording on one of the banners: *Mickelson—Perfect Vision in 2020.* What an interesting coincidence that the boy should mention his fortieth year—the same apparent year as this political rally.

Franklin stopped mowing and leaned over the handle for support. *The boy I saw drown in the river is the very same person I saw campaigning for president in the year 2020!*

But how could this be? The images were exact opposites! *Both* realities could not be true. Which was real? Which was true? What a staggering paradox!

Franklin almost yanked out a few tufts of hair in frustration. He'd have never pegged this boy as a future president of *anything,* least of all modern America. There had to be some mistake. Some misunderstanding or miscalculation. Tory Mickelson *couldn't* be the same person he'd seen at that rally. Yet Franklin recalled that the man on that platform was very close to forty years old. Could there be another youngster named Mickelson whose hometown was Elysia, Illinois, around thirteen years old, who nurtured presidential ambitions? The odds seemed outrageous. How might he find out for certain?

And if in fact both of these persons were the same, what fly in the ointment had created this ultimately confounding paradox? Franklin did not have to mow the lawn much farther before he came up with the most likely solution. He stopped again and voiced the answer aloud.

"The fly in the ointment . . . is *me!*"

. . .

Tory found Michalene engrossed in the *Encyclopaedia Britannica,* Macropaedia, volume 19, pages 556 through 559. Beside her sat the other volume Frank Benjamin had been reading, but she hadn't found the article on time nearly as revealing.

"I think you're letting your imagination get the best of you," Tory told his sister. "Frank is definitely weird, but I don't think he's an alien."

"*You* were the moron who suggested he was an alien," said Michalene.

"You got another suggestion?" asked Tory combatively.

"As I matter of fact I do."

She slapped the encyclopedia under Tory's nose. "This is the article Mr. Benjamin was reading last night before he fell asleep."

Tory glanced at the heading. "Benjamin Franklin? So what?"

"So *what?* Listen to this! '*Franklin was born in Boston, Massachusetts, on January 17, 1706, the 10th son of 17 children . . .*'"

Tory shrugged.

"You need more?" Michalene continued reading. '*At twelve he was apprenticed to his brother James, a printer.*'

Or this! ' . . . *after a bitter quarrel, Benjamin walked out.* . . . *Failing to find work in Boston or New York, Franklin proceeded to Philadelphia.*'"

Tory still looked perplexed.

Michalene drilled it home. "Do you remember our conversation at the breakfast table or was your brain in cryogenic storage?"

"So he has a lot in common with Ben Franklin. Big deal."

"A lot? Try *everything!* Even his name: Frank Benjamin. Don't you think it sounds a little *too* similar?"

"So what are you suggesting, Michalene? That Benjamin Franklin is outside mowing our lawn?"

"Of course not," said Michalene. "What I'm suggesting is that Frank Benjamin, if that's his real name, is totally obsessed with a man who lived over two hundred years ago—so obsessed he's actually memorized little details of Ben Franklin's life and applied those details to himself."

"Are you saying Frank is *really* nuts?" asked Tory.

"Think about it," said Michalene. "Insane asylums are full of people who believe they're George Washington, Marilyn Monroe, Benjamin Franklin—"

"Sometimes I wish I was Arnold Schwarzenegger," said Tory. "It doesn't mean I'm crazy."

"There's a fine line between wishing and believing," said Michalene. "I think Mr. Benjamin has crossed it."

Tory didn't buy it. "If he thinks he's Benjamin Franklin, how come he hasn't told us so? It's almost as if he's trying to hide the fact that he's insane. Is it possible for a crazy person to pretend they aren't really crazy?"

"I'm not sure," said Michalene. "Apparently so."

"Well, I don't care if he *is* nuts," said Tory. "I like the guy."

"I'm not saying we can't like him. Just because a person is sick, it doesn't mean they're bad or dangerous. But he needs help, Tory. Serious help. He might just need to know that people will accept him for who he is."

"So what's our next step, Dr. Freud?" asked Tory. "It sounds like first we have to tell him to stop pretending he isn't insane and admit that he thinks he's Ben Franklin. Then we have to tell him to stop pretending he's Ben Franklin."

"For the time being," said Michalene, "I think it would be better if we didn't tell him anything. We should just keep our mouths shut."

CHAPTER 7

A great burden had settled on Franklin's heart. Only one thing could be defined as completely out of place in this twentieth-century environment—himself. He didn't belong here. This was the only explanation he could fathom for the existence of two completely different and alternative realities. He recalled that the boy's death had been the last image he had seen before settling into the precise moment of August 24, 1993. This could mean that the vision he had seen first (the political rally) might be the *natural* reality, while the later image (the boy and the river) was somehow corrupt. It was only logical to believe that the corruption had been perpetuated by himself—by his own *un*natural intrusion into the twentieth century. *He* had caused the paradox. Such a concept left many unanswered questions. Franklin hoped to understand further when he read the accounts of his life and death at the college library.

The moment Franklin decided that he might be a factor in bringing about this boy's death, his first inclination was to run—to get as far away from Tory Mickelson as possible. By his absence, perhaps the succession of events that led to the drowning could be thwarted or avoided. But the philosopher was perfectly aware that the fuse might already be lit. The chain reaction that would lead to Tory's unnatural fate may well have been initiated the instant he knocked on the Mickelsons' door.

Franklin did not ignore the other conclusion: Perhaps the reality behind his vision of the boy's death was natural while that of the political rally was corrupt. But if this were the true course of nature, the course of nature deserved to be changed. Franklin had long ago abandoned the Calvinist notion of predestination. He could never accept the philosophy that man was destined to live out an unalterable future. To Benjamin Franklin, nothing was set in stone. He'd built his life on this conviction. The future was as malleable as a lump of clay. If this boy was destined to die, then Franklin would grapple with destiny. Franklin could never let Tory fall from that pipe knowing he had somehow been the cause.

But what could he do? How could he manipulate the future? Which adjustments in Tory's life might bring about the most relevant changes? It was obvious that there was much amiss in Tory's family. This had been the case long before Franklin had come onto the scene. Many of this family's basic values appeared misplaced and undefined. Could a restructuring of such values bring about the relevant changes in Tory's future?

To seek to implement such values on short notice was tremendously intimidating for Franklin. He was well aware of his own inadequacies—he considered himself to be far from perfect. Yet he had always considered his specific methods for self-improvement to be among the greatest gifts he could offer the future generation. He had even included such ideas in the last excerpts of his memoirs. At the time he wrote them down, Franklin had been convinced that such principles could shape a more positive destiny for any individual who practiced them—no matter what his circumstances. Might they also play a key role in shaping the future of Tory Mickelson? Might they be the means of saving his life?

As soon as he thought this, Franklin wondered if he'd ever entertained a more audacious and presumptive notion. For what principles did a man of his antiquated experience have that could possibly benefit a soul living in the twentieth century?

. . .

Franklin labored until almost three o'clock that afternoon. He mowed the grass, raked and gathered apples, and weeded the flower beds in the front yard. It had been decades since he had felt so invigorated. To work again! To feel clean air moving through healthy lungs! How vaguely he had appreciated his youth when it was first upon him. No wonder he had grown old! It was a well-deserved penalty for his ingratitude.

Franklin's clothing was drenched in sweat. Now appeared to be a good time to ask one of the children to escort him to that second-hand clothing store on Chestnut. He found the twenty dollar bill in the breast pocket of his T-shirt, knocked on the door, and voiced his request. Both Tory and Michalene agreed to accompany him.

"Do you know how to ride a bike?" asked Tory.

"A bike?"

Michalene had anticipated such a clueless response. It would be in perfect character with his "Ben Franklin" delusions.

"Is it difficult?" Franklin inquired.

"Not at all," said Michalene mischievously. "Why don't you take Dad's bike. He rarely rides it."

"Very good," said Franklin. "Show me where it is."

Michalene had been curious to see what Franklin would

do without any instruction at all, but Tory hopped onto his own Huffy Invader to offer a brief lesson before she could stop him.

"These are the pedals," Tory explained. "The speed on yours is already set, so don't worry about it. These are the hand brakes . . . "

Tory didn't feel the least bit self-conscious about having to explain such mundane details. He had accepted the idea that something was wrong with Frank, but he wasn't quite ready to call it insanity. Tory felt certain that Frank was perfectly aware of how to ride a bike. Surely he knew about *all* of this stuff, but something must have caused him to forget. He recalled Mr. Benjamin's disheveled appearance when they first met—charred clothes, bloody nose. Maybe the bump on the head or some other accident had afflicted him with a kind of amnesia. What if the last thing he saw before blacking out was an image of Benjamin Franklin? Tory rather enjoyed pretending Frank was from another century. It was good training in case Klingons ever landed in Illinois with a desire to learn about life on planet Earth.

As Michalene watched Mr. Benjamin take his first spill in the driveway, she decided to let her imagination run wild. What if this really *was* Benjamin Franklin? There was no harm in entertaining such a notion for a few moments. People had told Michalene so often that she was fat, nerdish, ugly, and unimportant, she had begun to believe it. Her only defense had been to prove that she was *smarter* than everyone else. Now that she was old enough to notice how boys looked at other girls and not at her, she was beginning to seriously question the value of her own intelligence. If some twist of fate could bring Benjamin Franklin—*the* Benjamin Franklin—to her home, it would prove that all those cruel, selfish, short-sighted people were wrong. *You didn't think I was important, eh? Well, how would you like to meet Mr. Benjamin Franklin?*

Frank's second spill, this time into the hedges, awakened Michalene from her fantasy. Mr. Benjamin was nothing more than a man with a serious mental illness. So serious that she wondered if she shouldn't just call the hospital and have someone take him away. It might be the most humane thing she could do.

"I think you're getting the hang of it," Tory told Franklin as he lay with his feet tangled in the bicycle. "You kept your balance almost twenty feet that time! You, sir, are ready to graduate to the street."

On the street, Franklin allowed Tory and Michalene to give him a push start.

"Pedal!" the children shouted. "Pedal!"

Franklin concentrated on holding the handle bars steady, repeatedly telling himself it was all a question of balance. His concentration was so intense that he failed to hear the kids yelling, "Turn! Turn!"

He collided with the neighbor's parked Ford Ranger. There was no damage to the truck, but as for Franklin, splayed in the muddy gutter, there were several nasty bruises on one elbow and both knees.

"That was great!" shouted Tory. "I've never seen anyone learn how to ride so fast!"

"Was that riding?" moaned Franklin. He was beginning to wonder how anyone survived in this century at all.

On his next attempt, Franklin finally caught the hang of it. He achieved a reasonable speed and then allowed himself to coast. With the wind in his hair, the Philadelphia philosopher was heard to shout, "Fantastic!"

He wondered how mankind had failed to invent such a device for so many millennia. Such methods of propulsion were so basic—so simple! Just pedals and gears! This instrument alone, thought Franklin—this Huffy Stone Mountain— would have absolutely revolutionized eighteenth-century transportation!

"Wait for us!" yelled the children. "The thrift store is the other way!"

As they raced into the Elysia city limits, Tory and Michalene continually challenged Franklin to increase his speed. Nothing failed to captivate his imagination—street lights, neon signs, the McDonald's arches, a giant billboard advertising a Caribbean cruise. People made a living in the most unthinkable occupations: selling car stereos, tropical fish, motor homes, oil and lube, music tapes, computers, and satellite dishes. Franklin could only guess at the purpose behind many of these goods and services, but he was anxious to try his hand at every one of them.

As they pedaled past a group of boys standing before an establishment called "Galaxy Video—Arcade and Rental," one of them signaled for Tory to stop. Franklin and Michalene waited a short ways up the sidewalk. Franklin thought these boys looked considerably older than Tory. They greeted the lad with much hand slapping and good-natured nicknames.

"Giles Peck," Michalene grumbled under her breath. *"Mega-creep."*

Franklin assumed she meant the tall boy in the center.

"Who's the old dude with the ponytail?" Giles asked Tory.

Franklin wasn't sure he liked being described as an "old dude." He looked at his reflection in the arcade window to be sure he was still thirty-two. Then he smiled. To an adolescent, *everyone* was old.

"Friend of the family," Tory answered. "He's staying with us a while."

As Franklin watched Giles, he felt a keen sense of recognition. Had he met this boy before? He couldn't imagine where. And then he recalled his first night in the twentieth century: the attack by that gang of ruffians. Of course! Now he recognized the voice—the outline of his head. Giles' hair was clipped so even and short it more closely resembled a coat of stiff fur. Why, these boys were little more than villains! Franklin wasn't surprised that they didn't seem to remember *him*. Their victims, no doubt, were chosen at random. He doubted very much he was their first target, or even their last.

"You still grounded, honcho?" asked Giles.

"Do I look grounded?" said Tory.

"Where you gonna be Friday night?"

"Right where you want me," Tory assured him.

Giles slapped Tory on the back. "Good man. Stay cool, kid!"

As soon as they'd pedaled out of the gang's hearing, Michalene said to her brother, "Why do you even talk to that jerk? He's just gonna get you in worse trouble than you're already in—or killed."

"He's my friend," said Tory. "Oh, but I forgot. You don't have any so you wouldn't know what those are."

"If he's your only one," said Michalene, "neither do you."

Franklin wondered what business Tory had been invited to participate in on Friday night. It couldn't be the kind of activity befitting a future president of the United States. He wanted to ask Tory about it, but decided it might be best to wait.

The thrift store on Chestnut was a smorgasbord of some

of the most unique and beautiful clothing Franklin had ever seen. Michalene asked the woman behind the register for a tape to measure Franklin's trouser and collar sizes. The woman volunteered to measure him herself.

"Did you sit in a mud puddle?" she asked.

"Indeed, I did," said Franklin. "And if you are seeking a place to sit, I'm afraid I cannot recommend it."

The woman laughed. "Looks like you scraped your elbow, too."

Franklin examined the drying blood. "Well, I blame these children. You see, they forewarned me that I would see a most beautiful woman at this establishment, and in my rush to get here I must have been a trifle clumsy."

The woman blushed and smiled. She was at an age when such compliments were most gratifying.

"A little old for you, isn't she?" asked Tory as they made their way back toward the men's department.

"Never underestimate the charms of an older woman," said Franklin.

The kids began thumbing through clothes. Excitedly, Tory yanked a pair of jeans off the rack.

"*Girbaud!*" he shouted. "Only eight bucks! We'll make you the hippest hobo in Illinois."

"He only has a twenty," reminded Michalene.

"Do you know how much these jeans would cost brand new?" said Tory.

"For eight bucks he could buy three different pair of another brand," Michalene argued.

"Oh, yes—" Tory turned to Franklin. "And as you can tell, my sister is a real expert on fashion."

"At least I'm not stupid enough to pronounce *Girbaud* with a *d*."

"Now, Tory," said Franklin. "I perceive that your sister's

expertise may far exceed the frivolities of foppery and fashion. Look closely one day and I think you might see how well-dressed she is in other more esteemed categories."

Michalene's heart stopped. *Insane or not, I love this man.*

"Did you get a degree from the University of Cornball?" Tory asked.

Franklin put his arm around the boy's shoulder and led him down the aisle. "I did not. But have you heard of Harvard and Yale?"

"Yeah, right," said Tory. "Harvard and Yale. That's a good one."

"Well," Franklin walked on, "the degrees were only honorary."

As Michalene watched them continue toward the fitting rooms, she shook her head in awe. It almost didn't seem right that Frank wasn't Franklin. If any crazy man deserved to be Benjamin Franklin, she decided it was him.

• • •

Feeling rather dapper in his Girbaud jeans and Ocean Pacific pullover, Franklin remounted his bicycle. He had also been able to afford another shirt and four pairs of socks. With such fine clothing, Franklin finally felt part of the twentieth century.

Tory took them home by a different route. The road paralleled the river. As Franklin gazed down toward the water, a foreboding settled over him. He recognized this river. His discomfort intensified when Tory turned to his sister and suggested, "Let's go down there."

"No, Tory," said Michalene firmly. "Let's go home."

"Just for a minute. I want to show it to Frank. C'mon!"

Tory turned onto a thin trail that led down toward a

spillway. Just below the spillway a railroad bridge stretched across the river. Franklin recognized everything. He had been here before. The memory made him shudder.

Franklin knew he must follow the lad. "Your brother seems determined for us to accompany him," he told Michalene.

"That's because my brother is morbid," she replied.

Reluctantly, Michalene pursued Tory down the trail. Franklin followed. After a short distance they abandoned their bicycles and wandered through a thicket of trees, finally arriving at a secluded area underneath the bridge. The spot overlooked a twenty-foot drop into churning waters. The mist rising from the spillway served as a natural air conditioner. Franklin was not surprised to see a pipe stretching sixty yards under the bridge to the other bank. As in his vision, the pipe was suspended by steel cables at ten-foot intervals. It came out of the ground right at the place they stood. Franklin peered down at the churning river. He'd once considered himself the strongest swimmer in all of England. Yet on his best day, he was confident those foamy waters would have drowned him like a rat.

Franklin stiffened when he noticed Tory performing a balancing act on the pipe. Actually, Tory was in no danger. For the first couple of yards, the pipe overran solid ground. But beyond that, any unwary acrobat would plunge into unforgiving depths. Tory balanced out as far as the first cables. There, just overlooking the edge of the cliff, the boy caught a cable in each hand and leaned forward. He stared down into the churning foam. Inches beyond where he'd planted his feet the pipe began to be wet and slick from the mist.

"Tory!" cried Michalene. "You're not being funny! Get down from there! NOW!"

"Don't blow a cork, Sis. I'm fine."

Franklin stepped forward. He reached out for Tory, ready to snatch him up if he didn't take the hand voluntarily. "I tend to agree with your sister," he said, struggling to control the nervousness in his voice. "Please come down." Franklin's only comfort was in the fact that Tory's shirt looked different from the one he wore when he drowned. This shirt was yellow. The other was red.

Tory rolled his eyes and took Franklin's hand. As the boy hopped down and approached the others, he announced, "I like this place."

"Well, I *hate* it," said Michalene.

"But it's so peaceful," said Tory. "The sound of the spillway is so . . . soothing."

Franklin perceived that this place was deeply significant to both children. He decided the significance must relate to their little sister, Carolyn.

"I wonder," said Franklin, "if this is not also a place of great sorrow."

The corners of Tory's mouth turned down. Defiantly, he said, "Not for me. Before the accident this was always the funnest place in all of Elysia—in all the world. I used to sit here and watch the spillway for hours."

"How did you know," Michalene asked Franklin solemnly, "that my sister died here?"

Franklin shook his head. "I ventured a guess. Might it be possible . . . Could you tell me how it happened? Did she lose her footing somehow? On the pipe?"

"No," said Tory defensively. "Carolyn would never have climbed up on the pipe. I always told her to stay away from it. She was too little."

"We don't know how it . . . " Michalene swallowed hard.

"Nobody was looking at her when she fell. We don't know if it was here or . . . further down or . . . "

Michalene's eyes moistened. Franklin put his arm around her. *How horrible,* he thought, *that the Mickelsons might lose two of their children in the very same location.* He wondered again if his vision had not been of the death of little Carolyn. No! It was not a five-year-old girl who had fallen from the pipe. It was Tory! Why did he allow himself to doubt? He desperately wanted to interpret this whole affair differently. Maybe none of his visions had any significance whatsoever! What if it was all a meaningless jumble of time and space? Such an idea was not without merit. It did, after all, render it unnecessary to explain any paradoxes.

Tory shouted, "Here comes a train!"

The rumble grew louder. Franklin stepped out from under the bridge. There it was! The machine from his vision that had nearly crushed him like an insect! The train served as a reminder that he could not pass off the visions as hallucinations. If the train was real, so might be everything else.

"What a glorious machine!" Franklin cried, although the children couldn't hear anything over the noise. He counted the boxcars—thirty-two in all. The locomotive screamed by. As the rumble faded, Franklin could not resist his next inquiry. "Is it possible to ride this vehicle?"

"You want to ride a freight train?" said Tory. "I don't know if they'll let you unless you work for the railroad. Don't tell me you've never seen a train before either."

"Well, I . . . " Franklin's efforts to hide his identity were becoming increasingly difficult. "I've never had occasion to ride one."

Tory passed it off with a wave of his hand. "No big deal. Mom took us into Chicago on the train once."

"I doubt very much it was not a 'big deal,'" said Franklin.

"Really," Tory insisted. "It was nothing special." Tory was growing impatient with Franklin's amnesia. He decided he might cure Franklin simply by scolding him. "Maybe it's time that you stopped playing this game, Frank—pretending you've never seen any of this stuff." Tory caught a scowl from Michalene. He softened his approach. "What I mean is, we like you just the way you are. We like *who* you are, Frank. And we wouldn't want you to be anybody else. Understand?"

"I would never dream of being anyone else," said Franklin. "I find such things intriguing because I have always considered myself a most natural inquisitor."

"A what?"

"A man who must continually swill at the fountain of life and knowledge. This has ever been one of my most fundamental governing values."

"Governing values?" repeated Michalene.

"Yes," said Franklin. "Our governing values define us as individuals. The pursuit of that which sustains our values defines our very existence. What values govern *your* life?"

Tory smirked to indicate that he thought it was a stupid question.

Michalene shrugged. "I don't understand."

"What in this life is most important to you?"

"Money," Tory proclaimed sharply.

"An insightful reply," complimented Franklin. "But are you certain it is money?"

"Absolutely."

Franklin indicated the pipe which crossed the river. He almost faltered, recalling his ominous presentiments concerning it, but the pipe offered such a convenient analogy.

"If a pot of gold doubloons were balanced upon this pipe in the very center, would you venture out to obtain it?"

"Of course not. I wouldn't be that stupid," said Tory.

Franklin was actually relieved to hear this reply.

Then Tory added, "I'd get a fire engine and drive it up the railroad tracks. Afterwards, I'd lower myself down in the bucket and grab the gold."

Franklin grinned. "Ah, but the pot is teetering. By the time you obtained such means, all your doubloons will have spilled into the current. No, your only hope is to walk out onto the pipe yourself."

"That's stupid. I would die."

"Then are we free to conclude that this may not be one of your governing values? You must ask yourself, what *would* cause you to venture out over that river? And then you must pattern your life in accordance with your answers."

Tory didn't want to admit defeat. "I'm still not sure I wouldn't go after the gold."

Michalene came up with one. "To know if there's a heaven. To know if my little sister is there. If I could know for sure, I think I might give it a try."

"A noble cause," said Franklin. "Once I bargained with a friend that when one of us should die, his ghost would visit the other and answer this question with finality. My friend died first and never fulfilled his end of the bargain, which at the time I thought remarkably rude."

The children laughed.

Franklin continued. "I am inclined to wonder if a pipe leading to such answers is not continually before each one of us. But 'tis one thing to aspire, quite another to embark. Most of us will generally weigh the sacrifice and decline."

Tory shook his head. "There's nothing, then. I can't think of anything that would make me want to go out there."

"I submit," said Franklin, "that if such an option were put to a parent whose child had thoughtlessly ventured out onto that pipe, and now that child clung to one of those cables in terror, the parent would not hesitate in making the attempt."

"Not *my* parents," said Tory. "At least not my dad."

"I think he might surprise you."

"The gold, though," nodded Tory. "I think Dad would go after the gold."

"So what would make *you* go out there?" asked Michalene.

Franklin thought a moment. "If out on that pipe rested a book wherein was contained all the wisdom of the world, and the secrets ensuring the happy progress of humanity, I feel quite certain I would venture the attempt."

"Don't you think those kinds of opportunities are always before us too?" asked Michalene.

Franklin's eyes emitted such warmth that Michalene's heart soared again. "I do," replied Benjamin Franklin. "However, in my vast impatience, I would still venture the attempt in my hopes to abbreviate the journey."

"I know another thing that might make me go out there," said Michalene. She weighed her next words carefully. "If I could know for sure who you really are, I think I would give it a try."

For the first time, Franklin wondered if this little girl had indeed figured something out. "My dear, sweet Michalene," Franklin began, "when I am ready to reveal this to you, I do not think you will have to attempt anything so hazardous."

Tory looked up at the darkening sky. "There's a storm coming."

Michalene groaned. "They say this has been the rainiest

93

summer in five hundred years. Floods up and down every river."

They climbed back onto their bikes and raced for home. When they were about halfway there, the droplets began to hit their faces. Tory urged them to pedal faster. He knew the worst of the downpour would shortly commence.

Less than half a block from home, the sky overhead ignited under a blinding flash of lightning. The deafening peal of thunder was nearly simultaneous. The earth shook all around them. Franklin did not see the bolt impact the street behind him, but he heard the crack and he swore he felt the heat. Glancing back, he caught a brief glimpse of a blackened patch on the asphalt. The children were terribly shook up. They tossed their bikes aside and virtually dove toward the front porch. Franklin moved no less slowly. He felt greatly relieved when the door had shut behind them.

"Did you see that?" Tory shrieked. He turned to Franklin. "If you'd been pedaling any slower, you'd be a french fry right now!"

Michalene continued to tremble. "I've never seen lightning strike the ground before. I can't believe how close that was!"

Franklin looked equally surprised. He'd been a student of lightning for most of his life, yet never had he experienced such close proximity with a single fulmination.

Just as everyone was ready to begin laughing off the tension, another deafening crack of thunder shook the house.

Tory went to the window. "I think it hit the house! The lightning just hit the house!"

"Is there a lightning rod affixed to this dwelling?" Franklin inquired.

Gerald Mickelson emerged from his den. He'd heard Franklin's question. "Yes," he replied. "Thank heavens."

"It's almost as if the lightning is *trying* to hit us," said Michalene.

"Now, don't be silly," said Gerald. "Lightning doesn't do that. It's not as if lightning has a mind of its own."

As Franklin gazed out the window, watching the rain start falling in torrents, he seriously wondered if Gerald's assessment had been wrong. Even if lightning did not have a *mind* of its own, could it have a *will* of its own? The events of the last few minutes left Franklin entirely uncertain. He felt inclined to correct Michalene's suggestion that the lightning had been trying to hit *us*. If any conclusion were to be drawn, it would be that the lightning had been trying to hit *him*.

CHAPTER 8

Throughout the night the children, in their frightened excitement, counted eight separate lightning strikes upon their house, all of which were captured by the lightning rod. The rod then redirected each spark into the soil and rendered it harmless.

When Bonnie drove into the driveway, she witnessed one of the strikes and swore that the copper rod projecting upward from the house was glowing hot. Gerald wondered if by morning the rod would have melted. The power to the house blanked out for an instant after every hit. Resetting the digital clock on the microwave proved futile. After each jolt the family members would stiffen and exclaim that they had never heard of anything like this happening before. The repeated attacks demolished the notion that lightning never struck in the same place twice. Bonnie was confident that she had a front-page story for the *Elysia Gazette*—if, of course, she could get anyone to believe her. No one dared venture outside. Even the dog slept in the laundry room that night.

Franklin expressed as much astonishment over the phenomenon as everyone else. However, he did not present his theory about why this might be happening. On one occasion he caught the most curious look from Michalene. The look suggested that she, too, wondered if Franklin might somehow be the cause of all this. Her expression showed astonishment, as if something she had formerly thought impossible about their homeless houseguest might actually be true.

But why would the lightning be so determined to strike him down, Franklin wondered. Had his gallivanting through the centuries transformed his body into a kind of electrical magnet? An ultimate lightning rod? Perhaps by breaching the barrier of time he had violated the most cardinal of all natural laws. Since lightning was to blame for having perpetrated the sin, perhaps its penance was the destruction of the sinner.

Franklin scoffed at himself. Such a theory *humanized* one of nature's most powerful forces. He refused to believe it. There must be another explanation. If lightning could set its vengeful sights on one single victim, then why not fire or water or wind? Would there be any safe haven left for him in the twentieth century?

Between power outages, Franklin spent a good part of the evening watching Tory display his skills at Super Nintendo. It proved to be a happy distraction from his broadening list of worries. Tory challenged him to a game of *Super Mario III*. Franklin agreed, at first with great reluctance and, for the first few minutes, with downright frustration. But toward the end of the evening he'd begun to show modest proficiency at the game, surviving on one occasion into the "Koopahari Desert" level until his computer entity was mercilessly annihilated by a tenacious fire snake. The flash whereby his entity was destroyed offered Franklin a sobering reminder of the danger that might await him the moment he stepped outside the front door.

Toward bedtime, Gerald entered the living room and suggested that, after tonight, Frank Benjamin should expect to sleep at the shelter. The children became almost hysterical in protest.

"If you make Frank sleep at the shelter, then plan on having me sleep there with him," said Tory.

"He can't live here forever," said Gerald.

"Why not?" asked Michalene. "Mom was thinking of hiring a live-in housekeeper anyway. Why can't it be Frank?"

"Don't be ridiculous," said Gerald. "Frank doesn't have any experience cooking or cleaning."

"He knows a lot more than you think," said Tory.

Bonnie overheard and stepped into the conversation. "For a few days or a week, I don't see any problem at all with Tory's idea. Besides, the forecast says it's going to rain all day tomorrow. He won't be able to finish the yard work we promised him until Friday or Saturday. If Frank wants to stay, he's welcome."

Bonnie glanced at her husband. Gerald's cheeks popped in and out—a sign that he was inwardly fuming. But there was nothing Gerald could do. He'd already agreed as part of the divorce to grant Bonnie the house. They would share joint custody of the children, but Bonnie would be the primary-care provider. They would live with *her.* She enjoyed showing Gerald how little influence he would soon have in determining the family's future.

Franklin was grateful for the generous offer, but he too could feel the husband's resentment. It might now be impossible for him to win over Mr. Mickelson's heart. Poor Richard's declaration that "fish and visitors smell in three days" came to mind. Two of those days were expended. Hopefully, he could disprove his own maxim.

· · ·

When Franklin awakened the next morning, his joints were stiff again. This time the pain was much more acute. Each muscle throbbed defiantly at any initial movement. Laboriously, he arose from the couch and began pacing the room. It took twice as long to work it out, but eventually the stiffness in his muscles and joints disappeared.

At breakfast he gently reminded Bonnie of her promise to allow him to sit in on her history class at the junior college. Bonnie had not forgotten.

"On Thursdays I stay on campus until about three o'clock," she said. "After American Heritage, I have modern dance, computer lab, and then Math 110. You're welcome to tag along to those as well."

"Regrettably, madam," said Franklin, "math, dancing, and, uh, computers were never my stronger suits. But I would very much enjoy visiting your library."

To Franklin's relief, there was only a light drizzle outside, with no visible electricity in the sky. Still, he emerged from the house with great apprehension, glancing timidly at the clouds. Nothing happened. Franklin sighed. Perhaps this paranoia had all been the product of his imagination. Was it foolish to consider that the repeated lightning attacks had been merely one of those freak occurrences that nature was occasionally wont to demonstrate? Whatever the case, no one looked forward to a clearing sky more than Benjamin Franklin. Unfortunately, the forecast in the paper called for a high probability of more thunderstorms that evening. Maybe as early as late afternoon.

Somewhat in keeping with the custom of his day, when passengers rode inside the carriage rather than up top with the driver, Franklin started to climb into the backseat of the Mickelsons' Bonneville. One queer look from Bonnie told him that sitting up front would be more appropriate.

He watched carefully as she poked the key in the ignition and turned.

"Ah, yes," said Franklin. He'd been curious to know how the engine's fire was ignited. He smiled at Bonnie to fend off another quirked expression. As they pulled into the street, he inquired, "Would it be possible at some convenient moment to be instructed on how to operate this machine?"

"Do you have a driver's license?"

"Driving requires a license?"

Bonnie grinned and shook her finger at him. "You're a real kidder, Frank. Have you *ever* had a driver's license?"

Franklin fumbled for a reply, "Where I am from, such a license was not, uh, available . . . required." He decided to be honest. "No, madam, I have never had such a license."

Bonnie frowned. "Please, don't call me *madam* anymore. It makes me feel like a little old lady shopping for shoes." She glanced at herself in the rearview mirror and tried to smooth the makeup deeper into her crow's-feet. She sighed dolefully. "Then again, if the shoe fits . . . I *am* forty-six. Maybe I should start acting my age."

"Nonsense," said Franklin. "In many ways my life did not begin until I was past forty." He bit his tongue. "That is to say, I do not *anticipate* that my life will begin until then."

"What I wouldn't give to be your age again," said Bonnie. "The older one gets, the harder it seems to start over. I'm sure you've noticed the tension in our house." She drew a deep breath. "Gerald and I are getting a divorce. There. I've told someone. I don't know why it's been so hard to confess. No one knows yet, except our attorneys. I haven't told my friends at work. We haven't even told the children."

"I'm very sorry," said Franklin. "Is there no way to avert this tragedy?"

Bonnie disapproved of his word choice. "I'd hardly call

it a tragedy. These days it's almost a status symbol. If you haven't been divorced, you're almost considered abnormal."

"Is divorce so common?"

"They say over half of all marriages end up that way anymore. I don't know why my marriage should have been on the better side of those statistics."

Over half! Franklin was shocked. Science and industry may have revolutionized the world, but he wondered if civilization itself—the beneficiary of this revolution—was on the decline. What had created such disturbing statistics? The number of children being raised under abnormal circumstances must be abhorrent. He recalled that in the London of his day, bachelorhood was in vogue. Among the patrons of British high society a gentleman who could successfully avoid matrimony was very much admired, almost revered. Franklin found such sentiments appalling—another symptom of corruption in the Empire.

He'd once written that marriage was the most natural state of humanity and therefore humanity's most likely course toward solid happiness. Any sentiment of conduct which interfered with the familial union represented the epitome of social disintegration. Jefferson's Declaration of Independence, as well as the Constitution of the United States, had been drafted on the principle that government could be tolerated only if it preserved the basic rights of life, liberty, and the pursuit of happiness. What if a society's attitudes toward what constituted happiness had become fundamentally corrupt? A constitution like the one they had drafted in the summer of '87 would hardly seem of much further use. It might simply become the guardian angel of immorality.

During the remainder of the drive to campus, Bonnie recounted all the reasons why she felt her marriage had failed and why divorce was justified. She and Gerald had married too young, she decided. He was twenty-four and she was twenty-two. Franklin raised an eyebrow. In his day if a woman were still unmarried by twenty-two it was generally thought she had something wrong with her. Bonnie also believed their courtship had been far too short. Franklin expected her to say it had been a few weeks. When she said nine months, again he was stymied. He knew of many marriages in colonial America in which there had been no courtship at all. Admittedly there were occasional disasters arising from such unions, but the majority of them, by all appearances, got along swimmingly.

Bonnie spoke of differing goals, conflicting opinions, and the failure of either spouse to meet the other's needs. She told how Gerald had changed over the years. Franklin thought she'd reveal how her husband had become disposed to fits of violence or drunkenness. No—she said he'd become self-centered, inconsiderate, and distant. Faults to be sure, but hardly the depravities Franklin had expected to hear. She was convinced that with Gerald she could no longer grow as a person—another concept that Franklin found utterly foreign.

Not that marriage in the eighteenth century was any easier. In Franklin's experience one of the more common crimes was outright abandonment. The first husband of Franklin's wife had been guilty of this atrocity. On his first voyage to England, Franklin had been accompanied by a man who was abandoning both a wife and young children. Years later, when Franklin returned to England, this old friend had approached him to report that he had a new family. He was genuinely frightened that Franklin might reveal his sin, thus destroying his current family and his reputation. The man cared little that he had already destroyed the reputation of his wife and children in Philadelphia. Franklin kept the man's secret, but he couldn't help but pity his friend. How could a creature of conscience live under such nail-biting nervousness and guilt day after day? To be sure, Franklin was not without his own sins, but at least he had taken responsibility for the product of such mistakes, foremost being his illegitimate son, William.

Franklin began to perceive that the entire concept of what one expected from marriage had changed significantly. People seemed less willing to adapt and much more determined to find a perfect fit from the outset—as if seeking a mate were like purchasing a pair of boots. No wonder divorce was such an epidemic! Commitment seemed applicable only as long as the other person continued to match the persona they had projected during courtship. As if in the course of human history this had ever been the case! As Poor Richard said, "Keep your eyes wide open before marriage, half shut afterwards."

In many ways he and his own wife, Deborah, had been as different as pot roast and porridge—in background, in education, in habit, in preferences—even in temperament. He could not deny that there had been scuffles, especially in the early days, but after forty-four years the faults of his Old Joan, if in fact she had any, grew virtually invisible. Had mutual acceptance become a futile objective? Had the phrase "for better or worse" been reduced to "for better or else"?

Franklin almost began dispensing marital advice, as he had done so often in his patriarchal years for friends like Madame Brillon in Paris. But in spite of all Mrs. Mickelson's comments, Franklin could tell that the divorce was not her decision. He perceived that in many ways her arguments had been developed to convince herself that Gerald's decision was the right one. Or perhaps she had simply accepted the inevitable and found such arguments comforting.

To Franklin it was obvious that Gerald Mickelson was succumbing to that restlessness that so frequently afflicts a man of middle age—a restlessness difficult to suppress if the proper values and self-disciplines have not been entrenched years beforehand. Franklin was so glad to be past all that. He was so glad that—

What was he saying? He wasn't past it at all! Had he forgotten his age? His newly acquired youth? Oh, heavens!

Perhaps the prospect of reentering the youthful world of romance and courtship would have delighted any other octogenarian, but Benjamin Franklin groaned within. He'd gratefully forgotten many of the unfortunate and reckless errors of his youth. Hopefully such errors would not be repeated the second time around.

. . .

As Franklin and Bonnie entered the lecture hall, the class instructor—a young woman—stood down front beside the podium, shuffling through her notes. Franklin would have been surprised enough to learn that the teacher was a woman, but this particular woman was also quite lovely.

A female instructor! *My,* how times had changed! In Franklin's century a woman was fortunate to be literate at all. Those who *could* write did so phonetically with little consideration for proper spelling. His own Deborah would close her letters with the words, "Your A Fect Shonet Wife, Debby."

As a young man Franklin had often advocated equal education for girls, but it had never occurred to him that the day might come when women would stand at the helm of intellectual discussion and debate. Although it was difficult to suppress a slight twinge of intimidation at such a prospect, he was nevertheless intrigued. American history as presented through the eyes of the gentler sex might prove uniquely compelling.

He sat with Mrs. Mickelson in the fourth to last row. Even from this distance he was taken in by his instructor's dazzling blue eyes. Her hair may have been slightly shorter than he preferred, pinned back tightly in a small bun, but that figure of hers, defined in a most flattering way by an austere yet undeniably feminine blue suit, was a positive show-stopper. During his walk across campus Franklin had found most of the current female fashions shockingly immodest. He had started to wonder if the twentieth century had entirely abandoned taste for ostentation. Ah, but here, at last, was a *lady*.

Franklin's commitment to ignore his natural impulses quickly faded. He decided that when the lecture was over he would ask Mrs. Mickelson to introduce him to the instructor. Perhaps he could interest her in a picnic or a stroll. How *did* gentlemen of the twentieth century strike up a courtship? The philosopher's sincerity and easy conversation had never failed him before. He hoped such skills might prove time-less.

Miss Chenoweth (that's what one of her students called her) began her lecture with a hasty review of the previous week's discussion on factors which led to the signing of the Declaration of Independence, including the Stamp Act, Lexington and Concord, and the Boston Tea Party. Franklin deeply regretted having missed that one. He would have been delighted to impart a few insightful anecdotes. Part of him was still very much an eighty-four-year-old man with an anxious need to ramble. Perhaps it was best that he had not attended. Poor Miss Chenoweth might never have completed her lecture.

Miss Chenoweth stated that the purpose of today's discussion was to dispel many long-standing myths about this period of American history, myths that had been perpetuated, she felt, by the Victorians of succeeding generations who, bless their hearts, did not cotton to some of the more plain, embarrassing, or downright scandalous facts surrounding the characters and events of the American Revolution. They, therefore, embellished many things, suppressed others, and ignored the rest.

Franklin settled into his seat. Miss Chenoweth's approach seemed sincere enough. Undoubtedly many myths had arisen out of the eighteenth century, just as they had arisen from every century previous. It was a natural, though unfortunate, tendency of mankind to present a false embellishment of its history and an unwarranted deification of its heroes. Such tendencies, left unchecked, could well lead to injustice and atrocity, as in the case of fanatical Christians who from time to time had found themselves promoting unholy crusades and bloody inquisitions under the false license of embellished history and interpolated doctrine. *The good Miss Chenoweth,* Franklin decided, *has spirit as well as beauty.*

"You may have to set aside many of the things you learned in grade school and junior high," Miss Chenoweth continued. "If history teaches us anything, it tells us that great things can be accomplished *despite* the shortcomings of its authors."

Hear, hear! thought Franklin.

"As we discussed last week, the Boston Tea Party had very little to do with rebellion against British taxation. The duty on British tea had actually been reduced in the colonies so that tea

106

exported by the British East India Tea Company, an institution near bankruptcy, could compete with the price of tea smuggled in from Holland by merchants like John Hancock. The Tea Party was therefore carried out by smugglers who wanted to keep the American tea market to themselves."

Franklin listened in fascination. He had argued from the outset that the dumping of three hundred crates of tea into the Boston Harbor was nothing less than a criminal act. He had urged the Boston patriots to repay the East India Company so that public opinion of the American cause would not suffer throughout Europe. He had even offered to pay the debt himself, out of his own private accounts! However, to say that the event had been conducted exclusively by self-serving smugglers, for their own gain, struck Franklin as slightly unfair. He was surprised that Miss Chenoweth did not go on to speak about the overwhelming inequities instituted by the British on American commerce and how smuggling in general had been perpetuated by these inequities.

"It's also a mistake," said Miss Chenoweth, "to assume that the cause of the Revolution had anything to do with the theme: 'taxation without representation is tyranny.'"

Franklin cocked an eyebrow. *Well, now, I'm not certain I would quite agree with that . . .*

"The fact is," Miss Chenoweth continued, "most Americans went without representation in their own colonial legislatures—let alone the British Parliament. Only white male landowners were allowed to vote anyway. Nor did the colonists really even *want* representation in Parliament. Oh, they complained about it endlessly, but this was only for the sake of propaganda. Outnumbered by the British representatives, they knew they would most certainly lose on every issue of vital importance."

Hmmm, thought Franklin. Most of her facts were accurate, but her conclusions seemed muddled. Representation in Parliament had been one of the principal objectives Franklin had struggled to obtain for over ten years while serving in England as an agent for the Pennsylvania Assembly. Franklin, at least, had believed that representation in Parliament would *very much* have made a difference. Such representation would have given Americans equal footing with British citizens—a distinction they never attained. The way it stood, Americans had no channel for the redress of grievances whatsoever.

Miss Chenoweth's statement that only white male landowners were allowed to vote was accurate, but misleading. Even when decisions were passed in colonial legislatures, they were frequently invalidated by Parliament. The real power in the colonies was held by the colonial governors, placed in office not by the vote of any American but by the arbitrary hand of Parliament, or, as in the case of Pennsylvania, by a proprietary family (the descendants of William Penn) whose chief concerns were not American rights, but continuing profits. (Franklin had tried in vain to convince Parliament that granting the one would forever ensure the other.)

"The Revolution," continued Miss Chenoweth, "is frequently misrepresented as a struggle between Americans and British foreigners. This, of course, is utter nonsense. In this respect, the Revolutionary War was much more like the Civil War. For the most part, it pitted Americans against Americans. We sometimes forget that almost as many Americans fought for Britain as fought against Britain. In 1780, when there were nine thousand patriots fighting beside George Washington, there were eight thousand Loyalists fighting against him."

Franklin nodded. She was correct, even if her point was a bit overblown. Not only had the Revolution pitted American against American, but as in his own case, it had pitted a father against his only living son, a fact that still pained Franklin to the very core.

"Americans don't like to remember their barbaric treatment of the Loyalists," Miss Chenoweth remarked. "Hundreds were tarred and feathered. Thousands were forced to relinquish millions of dollars in property without compensation. At least eight thousand fled to Canada and lived out the rest of their lives in poverty. But we don't talk much about the Loyalists. After all, they're the losers, right? And America hates losers, especially losers whose resistance didn't amount to much and who fought for such a useless cause."

Didn't amount to much! Franklin shifted in his seat over that one. There were atrocities committed on both sides. None could be excused, but why trumpet the one and ignore the other? His own son had instigated many atrocities against the patriots.

This wasn't turning out to be the lecture he had expected it to be. Had the pendulum swung so far in favor of fanatical patriotism that now it was necessary to swing it back to the brink of past-due shame and disgrace? Even with all the facts known, all the sins revealed, could future generations view the American Revolution as anything other than the glorious event that it was? Could the establishment of the first democratic government since ancient Greece and Rome be seen as anything other than extraordinary?

"But if you find our popular myths about the Revolution revealing," said Miss Chenoweth, "listen a moment while I demythologize a few of our more rakish Revolutionary heroes and founding fathers."

109

Oh, here we go, thought Franklin. If he didn't know any better, he might have suspected Miss Chenoweth to be a British spy.

Her first victim was a man named Paul Revere. Franklin had never heard of him. When Miss Chenoweth mentioned a connection between Mr. Revere and the town of Boston, Franklin thought perhaps he'd heard of a silversmith by that name. Miss Chenoweth reported that Revere's fame was largely due to a poem by a man named Longfellow and that he had never completed his famous midnight ride, having been cut seriously short when he fell into enemy hands near Concord. She also mentioned that during the war Revere had been reprimanded for cowardice while serving as a naval officer. Since Franklin was unaware of this man's military career or reputation, he had no way of judging Miss Chenoweth's assessment. On the next castigation, however, it was all he could do to hold his tongue.

"Thomas Jefferson, for nearly a century after his death, was viewed not so much as a founding father as a typical 'tell 'em only what they want to hear' brand of politician."

This was also the first time Franklin heard his own name mentioned. It was in connection with the Declaration of Independence. Miss Chenoweth stated that Benjamin Franklin was to have been the original author of the Declaration, but was passed over because his son was a British sympathizer.

"Hogwash," mumbled Franklin aloud.

His volume was low enough that only Mrs. Mickelson and several nearby students turned to look at him.

I was not passed over, thought Franklin. *I willingly declined.* And after watching Jefferson squirm over the mutilations inflicted upon that document by Congress, he was glad he did. Franklin was nevertheless proud of the contri-

110

butions he *had* made to the Declaration. For example, when Jefferson wrote "We hold these truths to be sacred and undeniable," he sharpened it to "We hold these truths to be self-evident."

Miss Chenoweth went on to say that Jefferson, like most of the founding fathers, was a "virtual atheist" and a sexual profligate, having fathered several illegitimate children by more than one of his Negro slaves. She also accused him of having resorted to bribery while president to keep one particular illicit affair under raps.

So Jefferson had become president! *Good for him!* cheered Franklin. As for the other matters, he knew that at least Jefferson called himself a Christian, although Thomas may not have been immune to occasional and healthy speculations on Christ's divinity. What honest Christian had not? As if faith were a thing more generally bestowed and not acquired! As to Jefferson's sexual improprieties, Franklin could only shake his head that history would take an interest in such a subject. No doubt by calling the emperor a whoremonger, the citizenry could feel free to happily go a-whoring.

After Jefferson, Miss Chenoweth started in on Washington. Franklin might have thought that America's venerable war hero would find himself beyond reproach. Not so. The audience was told to disregard the "cherry tree" story as utter fiction. She then advised everyone not to stand him up as an impregnable pillar of honesty, either. She accused Washington of being an "inveterate land-grabber" and told how as a young man he had illegally staked out prize territory west of the Allegheny Mountains in a region declared off-limits to settlers. She reported how as a general he had written several searing letters to the Continental Congress telling them they were unworthy of the services he was providing. She claimed there was evidence that Washington, too, had had an affair with a married woman and that he had been "an embarrassingly ineffective president." She even went so far as to report how much Washington had hated his own mother!

"Tea-party gossip!" Franklin scoffed aloud.

This time, twice as many heads turned to look at him.

To Franklin, such men as George Washington and Thomas Jefferson were not apparitions who had been dead for two hundred years. They were men he had seen and corresponded with only days earlier. It seemed quite cowardly to level accusations against men who had no means of defending themselves. Franklin wanted desperately to set this woman straight, but he was too keen a judge of character to waste the time. Such efforts would be futile. The lecturer obviously extracted a certain degree of pleasure from frolicking about in the mud, and few humans will ever allow logic or fidelity to separate them from their pleasures.

"But without a doubt," Miss Chenoweth continued, "the most misrepresented of all our founding fathers is Benjamin Franklin."

Franklin's face fell into repose. In the cause of his friends, he might suffer himself an undisciplined utterance, but during his own examination, he would keep his countenance immovable, as if his features had been carved of stone.

Even before the instructor began, Franklin tried to imagine what dirt she might have scraped together. *Of a surety she will mention my illegitimate son.* After all, his enemies had found this their favorite subject to leak whenever he ran for public office. He did not doubt that, in keeping with her theme, she would also try to raise eyebrows with a few examples of his more irreverent correspondence with lady friends. *In what other ways might history find me culpable?* He was in for some surprises.

"It seems that whenever a great writer has wanted to portray America as phony, materialistic, or lacking a soul, he or she has included references to Benjamin Franklin."

Franklin's face remained in repose. He was, however, somewhat perplexed by such a statement. What might have warranted this accusation?

"D. H. Lawrence, in reference to the overly simplistic quest for perfection that Franklin outlined in his *Autobiography,* wrote: 'And now I, at least, know why I can't stand Benjamin. He tries to take away my wholeness and my dark forest, my freedom. For how can any man be free without an illimitable background? And Benjamin tries to shove me into a barbed wire paddock and make me grow potatoes or Chicagoes.'"

My wholeness? My dark forest? My freedom? Who was this D. H. Lawrence? A poet, obviously. And as was typical of too many poets Franklin had known, they were often far more interested in creating new truths than in mastering the ones already extant.

"Franklin's emphasis on material success and the *appearance* of virtue over actual attainment has also earned him scornful comments from Mark Twain, Nathaniel Hawthorne, Herman Melville, and Ralph Waldo Emerson."

Material success? Virtuous appearance over actual attainment? How could they have possibly judged me to be so skin-deep? Franklin decided they had lifted a few scant lines from his autobiography and built from this a skeletal model. If Franklin had known his character would be reconstructed by future generations *solely* by that autobiography, he might have been somewhat more diligent in seeing to its completion.

No doubt it was the quest for perfection itself that had offended so many. Any man who publicly admitted such a feat held himself up for immediate ridicule. Franklin had known this from the beginning. After all, perfection was rarely a popular cause. As he once told his friends in France, if the rascals of this world only knew all the advantages of virtue, they would become honest through sheer rascality. The small-minded man will always view moral law as restrictive rather than liberating. That was why Franklin had directed his autobiography to the young. How many virtues might they attain before being overtaken by adulthood and disillusionment?

"But how does Franklin fare even in the *appearance* of virtue?" asked Miss Chenoweth. "Not very well, I'm afraid."

Of course not, thought Franklin. By *her* measuring stick, who could? What satisfactions could be gained by such vilifications? Miss Chenoweth was like the adolescent who still smarted over the deception that her parents were infallible.

"We all know Franklin's achievements in fields like philosophy, invention, science, statesmanship, diplomacy, and so on. The truth is, Franklin was no original in this. There are many men in the Enlightenment with résumés so long, and history is well aware of them."

I do not doubt it, thought Franklin.

"Just because Franklin wrote 'a penny saved is a penny earned,' it would be a mistake to consider him thrifty. Franklin believed in spending money, not saving it, and frequently shocked friends with his extravagancy."

You speak of later life, thought Franklin. Of what purpose is the amassing of fortune if not to enjoy one day a few convivial allowances?

"And speaking of Poor Richard, don't believe Franklin

was the author of all but a few of those maxims. Most of them were stolen from other books and almanacs."

I never stated otherwise. But stolen? He had not been aware that they were *owned.*

"It can be argued that Franklin failed in every single one of his virtues," said Miss Chenoweth. "But his most exaggerated virtue was his commitment to the cause of American independence."

Franklin's face remained in repose, but there was a slight widening of the eyes. She had now entered the realm of downright fantasy.

"On the eve of the Revolution he wrote that England still had 'the best constitution and the best King . . . any nation was ever blessed with.' Dixon Wector, author of *The Hero in America,* wrote of Franklin: 'He kept his foot in the door of conciliation so long that it nearly got pinched.' When Parliament passed the Stamp Act he actually supported it! That is, until a mob threatened to burn his house down, after which his opinion speedily reversed."

Franklin marveled. Every bit of it was false and twisted.

"He apparently viewed his ambassadorship to France during the Revolution less as a diplomatic mission and more like a ten-year vacation. John Adams wrote that when he arrived in Paris the records and accounts of the American mission were in complete disarray. Adams intimated that Franklin spent more time leaping from bed to bed than he did negotiating with the French."

At last, Franklin burst out laughing. The disturbance caught the attention of the entire auditorium. Even Miss Chenoweth lost her train of thought.

"Pardon me," Franklin apologized, and then he exploded with another fit of laughter to the point where tears appeared in his eyes. He wondered if he should be flattered that the oft-times self-righteous Adams would suspect a man of seventy-five capable of so much energy.

"Sir, are you enrolled in this class?" Miss Chenoweth demanded.

"I am not, madam," said Franklin.

Bonnie added hastily, "He's considering it."

Miss Chenoweth spoke sternly. "I would appreciate it if you could control your outbursts."

"I apologize." Franklin suppressed one last guffaw and wiped away a tear.

Miss Chenoweth continued. "It's unfortunate that we have allowed ourselves for so long to be hoodwinked by the notion that our founding fathers were such pinnacles of faith, fortitude, and old-fashioned family values. Rarely has there been a more dishonorable husband and father than Benjamin Franklin. There are numerous examples of infidelity and lechery, some of which he freely confesses in his *Autobiography*."

Utterly amazing, thought Franklin. Because he'd confessed such follies from his youth, was he to be judged a slave to such vices throughout his life? Apparently, in the eyes of history there was no such thing as repentance or rectification. The man at eighteen was the same man at eighty.

"His only son was, after all, illegitimate," said Miss Chenoweth.

At long last! thought Franklin. *I thought you'd never bring it up.*

"There were very likely a half dozen other illegitimate Franklins as well."

There were?

"For the last twenty years of her life, the time Franklin spent with his wife can be counted, not in years, but weeks. Deborah Franklin died heartbroken in 1774, begging her husband to come home so she could see him one final time. He chose, instead, to stay with his mistress in England. Even the illegitimate son he raised ended up a victim of his neglect and wrath. If we don't know much about the real Benjamin Franklin, it's because the Victorians of the nineteenth century found him too much of an embarrassment and worked hard to suppress some of the racier tidbits. What remains of Benjamin Franklin is our familiar caricature of a little balding fat man in spectacles, flying a kite."

Not since Lord Wedderburn's castigation of Franklin in the Cockpit of Whitehall shortly after the Boston Tea Party had Franklin felt subjected to such abuse and humiliation. But the incident in the Cockpit was in the face of a stubborn and corrupt Privy Council—this was in the face of history! Or at least someone's myopic and warped perspective of history. Pray to God it was not the only perspective.

Mrs. Mickelson glanced over at Franklin again. Franklin's expression had fallen back into serene repose, but now there was a distinct air of sadness about it.

"Are you all right, Frank?" Bonnie asked.

"Yes," said Franklin. "I'm as fine as ever." Then he looked carefully about the room. "But as for these fine young people who have paid good money to listen to such rubbish, I am sorely tempted to weep."

One thing was for certain. Franklin no longer felt much of an inclination to ask Miss Chenoweth out on a picnic.

CHAPTER 9

"Well, Sis, you've finally flipped," Tory declared. "I knew it was just a matter of time."

"Don't you think I know how crazy it sounds?" said Michalene. "Can you try to open your mind for just one minute?"

Tory turned as if to leave. "I can't *listen* to this! If I listen, they'll lock *me* away right along with you!"

Michalene grabbed her brother's arm. "Tory, *please.*"

Tory spun back. "Just tell me one thing. If Frank is actually the *real* Benjamin Franklin, how did he get here? Did they have *Back to the Future* Deloreans back then?"

"How could I possibly know?" said Michalene. "All I know for sure . . . at least all I can *suspect,* is that it has something to do with lightning."

"Lightning?"

"Remember how it tried to get him when he was riding the bicycle? Tory, I've never known lightning to hit our house even when Frank Benjamin *wasn't* staying with us. But eight times in one night? Do you know what the odds of that are?"

"Why would that prove Frank is Benjamin Franklin?"

"It's just the final piece in a very bizarre puzzle. It proves that there's something, well . . . metaphysically *wrong* with him. Something that most likely happened when he traveled forward in time."

"Something that affected the *weather?*"

"Why is it so inconceivable?" asked Michalene. *"You're* the science fiction nut."

Tory shook his head. "I just . . . I just can't—"

"Look at the pictures," said Michalene. "Look at *all* of them."

On Michalene's bed lay four different paintings of Benjamin Franklin, including one Norman Rockwell rendition of Benjamin Franklin as a young man standing in a blacksmith shop and overseeing the construction of the first Franklin stove. Michalene had clipped the pictures out of various books in the family library.

She watched her brother place each picture up to his nose. "Do you see the resemblance?" she asked.

"I don't know. Maybe." Abruptly, he threw the pictures back on the bed. "Michalene, it just doesn't make sense! If he's Ben Franklin, how come he knows about things that the *real* Ben Franklin wouldn't have known until he was an old man? Like getting honorary degrees from Yale and Harvard?"

"We don't know how old he was when he got those degrees," said Michalene.

"How would he have even recognized himself on that hundred dollar bill?"

"Well, it does say 'Franklin' right on it."

"For all Ben Franklin might have known at thirty-two years old, that name could have meant *Mortimer* Franklin or *Lucretius* Franklin or even Franklin *Delano Roosevelt!*"

Michalene opened her mouth to answer, then she closed it again. *Wow.* Tory might have a point there. At thirty-two Franklin wouldn't really have known that he would play any major role in history at all. Michalene sat back on the bed and stared off into space. Then she clenched her hair in both fists and shrieked in exasperation.

Tory patronized her with a pat on the back. "Keep working on it, Sis. In the meantime, you might wanna call in to one of those 900-number psychiatrists."

Tory left the room. Michalene lay back on her bed, crushing the Franklin pictures beneath her. A corner of one of the cut-outs curled up into her face. She yanked the paper out from under her head, crumpled it violently, and prepared to toss it across the room. Then she stopped herself and carefully uncrumpled it again, glaring at the portrait.

"No," she mumbled aloud. "I'm right. I *know* I'm right. I just can't explain it."

There was only one option left. She would have to confront Mr. Benjamin Franklin outright.

• • •

He died at eleven P.M., April 17, 1790.

The biographies were quite clear. He died with his family at his bedside. One account stated that Polly Hewson had performed the last offices for the corpse. There was even a picture of Franklin's deathmask! Franklin reread the account several times. He was speechless. He nearly stood up and shouted, "It's all a grand hoax! I'm here! I'm alive! I'm in the twentieth century!"

How could history have reported on events that never transpired? He could not have died at eleven P.M.! Eleven P.M. on an equivalent time scale was the approximate time when he had been accosted by that gang of ruffians.

I was not there to have died! My face was not there for the molding of a deathmask! My corpse was not present to have had first, last, or any offices in between performed upon

120

it! Thank heavens he was not standing at the present site of Christ Church cemetery in Philadelphia, Pennsylvania. At the risk of arrest and incarceration, Franklin would have madly commenced excavating his own grave site, desperate to prove that the worm-rotted coffin was perfectly empty. There would be no bones, no dust, no evidence whatsoever that a body had ever lain inside. How his family had pulled off this fraud he did not know. Perhaps in utter shame at the fact that he had disintegrated himself inside one of his own inventions, they had bribed the appropriate doctors, morticians, pallbearers, and sculptors. Such persons then kept this secret to their graves to preserve the honor of Benjamin Franklin's memory. Succeeding at this kind of conspiracy would have been no less than a miracle!

He had no choice but to face the more staggering possibility. What if there *were* bones in that grave? What if he *had* died at eleven P.M. on April 17 of the year 1790?

If this were the case, he was left with two conclusions, either of which seemed riddled with incongruities. First, there was always the possibility that he would eventually return to April 17, 1790, and fulfill the requirements of history. In other words, at precisely 11:00 P.M., Benjamin Franklin would die.

Fine. Such a destiny seemed perfectly plausible. But the theory did nothing to explain why an alternate reality had already been recorded in the various biographies. As it stood, all the history books should have reported that Franklin's body had disappeared or disintegrated. Only *after* his return should twentieth-century biographies have read any differently.

Franklin's other conclusion was much more baffling, but regrettably, more logical: There were *two* Benjamin Franklins. There were also two Philadelphias, two planet

121

Earths, and two April 17, 1790s. As absurd as this sounded, Franklin's meager understanding of "hypertime" and "multi-dimensional space" as described in the article on time in the *Encyclopaedia Britannica* seemed to give such a paradoxical notion some credibility. Somehow, as Franklin cavorted through the years, his body had crossed over to an alternate reality—another realm of existence virtually identical to the one he had left. It was obvious that *something* like this had happened. Otherwise, how would he have seen the paradoxical visions of the destiny of Torrence Mickelson?

According to that *Britannica* article, the number of alternate realities that might exist in the universe was infinitesimal. In other words, the differences between himself and that man whose remains now lay in Franklin's tomb might have been so subtle as not to merit mention. For all practical purposes, he and the Franklin who had died at 11:00 P.M. on April 17, 1790, were the same exact person, except that one of them had managed to reach the chamber that morning as the lightning struck the rods, and one had not. Or perhaps the one whose remains now lay in the tomb had never constructed any kind of "rejuvenation" chamber in the first place. He had always thought it a kind of miracle that he had even found the time and energy to put it together.

So what conclusion could Franklin draw from all this—especially with respect to Tory Mickelson? It was now clear that even if Tory fell from that pipe and drowned in the river in *this* reality, there would always be another reality in some distant dimension where he would not, and thus go on to fulfill his destiny as a candidate for the presidency of the United States. So why should Franklin interfere? Whatever happened was bound to happen anyway. Right?

Wrong. Franklin would never acquiesce to such a fatalistic perspective on life. Such a perspective would undoubtedly engender the same temptation toward inaction that he felt was promoted by the doctrine of predestination. Whatever else might be true, Franklin had to accept the fact that this was now *his* reality. What he made of himself in it was still up to him. If he willingly allowed Tory to fall to his death, guilt would squarely rest upon his shoulders.

Might there be such a thing in the eyes of mankind's most Supreme Friend as "correct" realities and "failed" realities? Not two weeks ago, as Franklin had gazed upon his picture of the *Day of Judgment* at the foot of his sickbed, he had amused himself with speculations about how such an event might be conducted. He'd even wondered if the sinner might be shown in vision how his life could, should, and would have been different if, at certain intervals, he had made wiser decisions. Might this be one practical use for the existence of alternate realities as anticipated by modern science? As a kind of library for visions at the day of judgment?

Franklin felt a headache coming on. He almost wished he had not read that article on time. No wonder the acquisition of knowledge sometimes made men look back nostalgically to their days of blissful ignorance. Why was it that advances in human understanding always seemed to breed more questions than they answered?

He searched all the biographies in vain for any mention of his having constructed the chamber. Perhaps he was right to have assumed that, in this reality, it had never been built. He recalled having instructed his grandson, Benny, to wait ten years before disclosing any information relating to the chamber. After perusing the various biographies for three-and-a-half hours, Franklin discovered one likely reason why no account of the chamber existed. To his dismay, he learned that his grandson, Benjamin Franklin Bache, had died of yellow fever on September 10, 1798, at the age of twenty-nine—just nineteen months short of the date he was to have released all pertinent papers on the chamber. So what had happened to those papers? If they existed at all, such papers had apparently been misplaced or destroyed—lost forever to the world.

Reading the account of Benny's untimely death heightened Franklin's interest in learning the fate of everyone else he had loved and cared for, particularly the members of his immediate family.

He was disgusted to learn how his grandson, William Temple, had forfeited the estate he had inherited in New Jersey. Franklin had left it to him on the condition that he end his avowed bachelorship and take a wife. The record stated that Temple had not married until a few days before he'd died. Franklin had also willed to Temple his manuscripts and letters. These memoirs should have been a veritable gold mine for Temple. Yet he procrastinated the publication of any portion of them for twenty-seven years, finally producing only a partial sampling. William Temple Franklin—a man torn all of his life between a father, a grandfather, and the cultures of three different countries—finally died in Paris in 1823, succeeding at no other objective than to forever disappoint the expectations of those who loved him.

Franklin was pleased to hear that his daughter, Sally, shortly after his death, had finally sailed to England, as had always been her dream. When she was a young girl, Franklin had wanted to take her there, but, alas, his wife had objected. He was saddened to hear that Sally had spent the last fourteen years of her life on a country estate in remote Delaware. Franklin knew such seclusion from busy Philadelphia would have left her terribly lonely in her final years.

He knew that his sister Jane's last and greatest anxiety was that she would outlive her famous and loving brother. According to the accounts, she outlived him by four years.

As Franklin came across each account of the death of a loved one, he was stricken by acute pangs of grief, as if he had been present at the funeral or had just received notice from the postman. But for some inexplicable reason, no account of a loved one's death struck him more profoundly than that of his firstborn son, William. At first Franklin was rather surprised to find tears welling up in his eyes. After all, no person in Franklin's life had ever hurt him so severely or inspired such keen sensations of anguish.

He felt his breast pocket, looking for a handkerchief. Having none, he wiped his eyes on the sleeve of his shirt. For a moment he was convinced that his tears had been caused by those odd electrical lights in the library's ceiling, one of which was buzzing and flickering. Certainly the tears could not be for William. Over the past several years, any thoughts of his son had aroused in him only feelings of the coldest enmity. And yet he could feel his eyes moistening again. Why?

He abandoned me, Franklin reminded himself. *He betrayed me and took up arms against me in a cause wherein my good name, fortune, and life were all at stake.* And then the final blow!—just after the war had ended, when rapprochement might still have been possible, William followed up his formal offer of reconciliation with a scandalous attempt to entangle his son, Temple, in an embarrassing blackmail scheme. William arranged for Temple to unknowingly deliver clandestine information to a former American double agent in France. Using his only son as a pawn for political intrigue and financial gain! For Franklin, it was the last straw.

In spite of it all, he could not deny that he was weeping. Perhaps it was the poignant account in one of the biographies of William's unfruitful and insignificant final years. All of William's dreams appeared to have been shattered, all of his fortunes depleted. The book reported that William Franklin had died in London in 1814, professing to be an "injured soul" to the end of his days. Franklin was not surprised to read that Temple had heaped upon his father the same disappointments that William had heaped upon *him*. The betrayal had gone full circle. All of the misery that Franklin had once hoped for his son during his moments of deepest bitterness had come to pass. But if that was so, why did Franklin feel no satisfaction? Why, in his moment of vindication, did he feel only remorse for ever having wished such a curse upon his own flesh and blood?

Suddenly Franklin did not recall a single incidence of his son's offense. Had he been asked at this moment to try to divulge one, even a single one, he would have merely shaken his head and skewed his eyes in an effort to remember. The only images of William he saw at the moment were the happy ones—William the eager, keen-minded child, William the young man who skirted across the rainswept field with Franklin's silk kite, William the dashing military officer who journeyed with him into the Pennsylvania wilderness to defend the settlers against the Indians, William the faithful companion who had sailed with him on his second voyage to England. The adventures, the good times, the laughter. Ten years earlier Franklin had chosen to block out these images. With the confirmation of William's death, the sweet memories flooded back into his mind like water through a breached levee.

I did him wrong, the inexorable philosopher at last confessed. *He did* me *wrong to be sure, but, alas, I can lay no claim to better behavior.* How easily Franklin had put out of his mind the one issue that had caused the major embarrassment and torment of William's life—to know of his own illegitimacy and to endure a lifetime of hushed whispers and suppressed snickers.

Whatever mistakes his son may have made, it had not been a father's place to impose punishment. He felt ashamed that it had taken an account of his son's life and death to jolt him to the realization of his own crime. More painful to Franklin was the realization that the time of restitution, the day of forgiveness, appeared to have passed.

That blinding acid called pride! As he had once remarked, pride is the last vice a good man gets clear of. But though he had written it, he had not escaped it. If he was to be perfectly honest, the principal injury his son had inflicted upon him was embarrassment—to his reputation, to his politics, to his pride. All those things which Franklin had accused his Tory son of trying to deprive him of—property, fortune, influence—were gone now anyway, and suddenly they seemed rather inconsequential.

Franklin could only hope that somewhere out there, in the bosom of nature's God, his son could be made aware that his father's frozen heart had begun to melt. He also hoped that somehow William would hear the whisper that fell from his lips after the tears had subsided and the pages of the last biography before him had been closed.

"Billy, my son, I miss you and . . . I love you."

CHAPTER 10

The first sound that greeted Franklin as he emerged from the library was a toll of thunder in the west. He froze. He saw lightning out there too. The storm rumbled closer and closer, like warships testing the range of their cannon. Franklin had been so caught up in his studies that he'd lost track of time. It was now ten minutes after 3:00. Mrs. Mickelson would be impatiently waiting for him in the parking lot. The Bonneville had been parked just east of the Administration Building. For Franklin it was a five-minute walk—but only a two-minute run.

He took off down the cement walkway, dodging the young students and their knapsacks as best he could. If he could have, he'd have avoided close proximity with other people altogether, for fear that a bolt of lightning might spell doom for them all. Franklin estimated that there might be just enough time to reach the safety of the car. Could lightning pinpoint a single vehicle moving so swiftly? *Of course it could,* he realized. But perhaps while the car was moving, the lightning would be less accurate in setting its sights. He was further comforted by his postulation that even if lightning hit the car, the riders inside would not be grounded and would thereby avoid electrocution. In the driveway at the Mickelson's house his only moment of danger would occur as he sprinted toward the front door.

As Franklin dashed toward the parking lot, he heard more thunder. The storm would be overhead in minutes. When he reached the Administration Building, he took a shortcut across the lawn, ignoring signs to "Stay Off the Grass." Administrators in the first-floor windows glanced at him disapprovingly.

The first heavy raindrop hit Franklin's nose as he rounded the building. Drawing a breath, he rushed onto the pavement. But where was the car? There were *hundreds* of automobiles! It had never occurred to him to make a mental note of the car's location. Seeing hundreds of cars together like this, they all looked the same. *Her car was blue. Yes, dark blue and longer than average.* As he sprinted up one row of vehicles and down the next, he again felt grateful not to have been born in the twentieth century. How could the owners of automobiles possibly keep track of their property? As disorganized as Franklin considered himself, he had no doubt that losing his car would have been a regular hazard.

At the next peal of thunder, he stopped and closed his eyes, concentrating. He opened them again. Now he remembered. He and Mrs. Mickelson had crossed one perpendicular row of cars before stepping between a vertical row and then onto the walkway. Franklin found his bearings. He felt certain the car would be in the next row over.

It started to rain heavily. He moved anxiously down the line. It wasn't here! None of the cars on this row was even blue! Would Bonnie have left without him? If she did, Franklin knew he was a dead man.

A car honked. He looked around. There it was! But it wasn't Bonnie driving the blue Bonneville. It was Gerald. Franklin did not concern himself with that. As he dashed toward the car, the passenger's side window rolled down.

"Let's go!" Gerald called out.

Am I not moving fast enough? Franklin yanked open the door and leaped inside.

"I'm in!" he cried. "We should start moving."

Gerald calmly pressed the button and rolled up Franklin's window. He maneuvered through the parking lot and pulled into the street.

"They asked Bonnie if she could work early today," Gerald explained. "She came home about one o'clock and asked me to pick you up."

"I'm very glad that you did." Franklin was surprised that Gerald had agreed to come, considering the animosity he had displayed the previous night.

As the car picked up speed, Franklin started to relax. For the next several blocks, Gerald drove away from the storm. The rain on the windshield let up a bit.

"I thought this ride might give us a chance to get better acquainted," said Gerald.

"That would be delightful," said Franklin. He continued to watch the clouds. "I would very much enjoy hearing more about your work. What you told me yesterday sounded fascinating."

"Well, Frank," Gerald began, "it's *you* that *I* find fascinating. The way you stumbled onto our family. The way you seem to have won over my wife and children. You must be a pretty remarkable guy."

"You're very kind." Franklin now suspected that Gerald was using this opportunity to communicate some sort of ultimatum.

"I thought this might be a good time for us to talk man to man," said Gerald.

"Please do."

"Let me ask you something, Frank. What would it take to get you to move on?"

"Pardon me?"

"Tell you what. I'll give you three hundred dollars and a bus ticket to anywhere you want in the continental United States."

Franklin looked uneasy. To leave now might spell doom for Gerald's son. But how could he possibly explain this to Gerald?

"Your offer is most generous," said Franklin. "What have I done to merit such generosity? If I have offended you in some manner, I offer my humblest apologies." He continued to look off in the sky for flashes of lightning.

"No, it's not that. It's just—things are sort of out of kilter right now. I don't know if Bonnie told you, but she and I are in the process of divorcing. I'm supposed to move out next week. I've already signed a lease on an apartment across town. I wanted to make this as simple as possible, but . . . I guess this kind of thing is never simple."

Franklin tried to read Gerald's thoughts. "And you fear I might be complicating matters?"

"No," said Gerald. "Well, yes. Sort of. Oh, I don't know. I guess I . . . I guess I just didn't expect to have another male move in and take my place so easily. You know what I mean?"

"I'm sure that could not happen," said Franklin. "It sounds as if you might be having second thoughts about this divorce."

"Second thoughts?" Gerald shook his head. "No, nothing like that. I have regrets. I'll admit that. It's just not working, Frank. There's more to it than I could ever explain. We're just not happy. I think we married too young."

There it was again. That "too young" hypothesis.

"In my observation," said Franklin, "the earliest marriages have stood the best chance for happiness." He became

131

distracted by a lightning flash in the distance. He counted the seconds until the thunderclap. Four seconds. The storm was catching up to them again.

Gerald huffed in disagreement. "Maybe back in the dark ages. Today it's a whole different ball game."

"How so?"

"People have changed. *Women* have changed."

"I see."

"Don't get me wrong. Bonnie is a great lady. In the last fifteen years we've just become two different people."

"Are you open to a kind bit of fatherly advice?" asked Franklin.

"Fatherly advice? From you? I'm forty-eight years old, Frank. If I were a few years older, I could be *your* father."

Oh, dear, thought Franklin. To lose the advantage of age when dispensing advice was indeed a handicap.

"Then, as a friend, might I suggest that great ladies are much harder to come by than a man whose 'horse has been out of the running' for so long might suspect."

"Well, I wouldn't exactly say my 'horse' is out to pasture."

"*Rejoice with the wife of thy youth,* as the Good Book says," Franklin proclaimed. "As one grows older he tends to appreciate with a much weightier affection those who can smile at the same memories or join with yours the tears that fall when reflecting on moments more sorrowful."

Gerald nodded a few times, then his expression soured. "Are you married, Frank?"

"Not at present."

"Well, those are nice thoughts," said Gerald. "They're just not practical. Unless you've actually seen it from the inside out, I'm afraid you just can't know what I'm talking about. Believe me, these kinds of things are complicated."

Franklin sighed. *Complicated.* The final refuge of a weak argument.

Franklin had often observed that young people will grudgingly tolerate the rambling advice of an old man. Although they might deny its effects for the present, such advice, after a period of gestation, usually takes root. Franklin hadn't had much opportunity to observe the effects of advice imparted from young to old, but he suspected that pride might render such advice ineffectual.

From the beginning, Franklin had worried that the news of his parents' divorce would be the principal factor which enticed Tory to venture out upon that pipe. To save the marriage might save the boy. Of course, Franklin's interference in the Mickelsons' lives might also factor into the boy's death. What was the right thing to do? Whatever might be right, playing the part of marital sage for Mr. Mickelson appeared futile. Gerald's mind was set.

The car stopped at an intersection. Franklin looked up nervously at the clouds. There was lightning overhead. Rain pelted the windshield again. Gerald increased the wiper speed.

"Must we stop here?" Franklin inquired.

Gerald pointed at the stoplight. "It's red."

Another lightning bolt discharged in the sky. This time only two seconds elapsed until the thunderclap came.

"Looks like another stormy evening," Gerald observed. "Hopefully we'll have less excitement than last night."

Franklin squirmed in his seat. "What is the usual duration of these red lights?"

"This one? Minute or so. Why?"

Franklin noted that there was no traffic. "And what would happen if we were to charge right on through?"

Another lightning flash. The accompanying thunderclap was almost immediate.

"If you're worried about getting struck," said Gerald, "there's no need. Our tires would keep us insulated. Not that I've ever heard of lightning striking a car."

As if in revelatory denunciation of Gerald's statement, the heavens discharged again, and the lightning bolt zapped the streetlight directly above the Mickelsons' Bonneville. The bolt shattered the streetlight's metal arm. Multiple appendages of electrical fire branched off from the impact point, dissipating all across the ground. Gerald exclaimed a profanity. A shower of sparks rained on the Bonneville's hood, followed by glass and plastic shards. Larger chunks just missed the roof and windshield, crashing on the pavement. All four stoplights at the intersection shorted out.

"Go!" Franklin shouted.

Gerald hit the gas. The car spun its wheels in the water and tore off down the street.

"What is happening to the world?" Gerald cried. "Has nature gone mad?"

"Get us home! Quickly as you can!"

Gerald nodded. They were only about three blocks away. As the car rounded the next corner, another powerful blast of electricity hit the pavement directly ahead. Gerald swerved. Franklin gripped the hand hold on the door. The Bonneville hydroplaned, performing a one-hundred-eighty-degree spin in the middle of the street. An oncoming driver pressed his horn. The other vehicle stopped inches short of plowing into Gerald's door. On the street where the lightning had struck, the water had turned to steam.

Gerald was now a believer. The lightning was trying to kill them! He hit the pedal again, pulling a tight U-turn. The Bonneville nearly fishtailed into another spin. Gerald drove the final blocks in a serpentine pattern. A bolt of lightning struck on the right, and then on the left. It was like dodging missiles in a war zone!

Gerald turned into the driveway. The wheels screeched. He slammed on the brakes, skidding to an angled stop. The left front tire dug a trench in the lawn. Gerald kept the car running for a moment. He leaned over the steering wheel, panting, sweat streaming off his brow.

Franklin glanced out his passenger-side window and up at the clouds. His eyes came to rest on the exact point in the sky from whence the heavens hurled its next bolt of lightning, like watching the strike of a deadly serpent. A direct hit on the car's roof! The Bonneville became enveloped in waves of electrical fire. The engine stalled. The windshield wipers stopped. The dashboard darkened. Gerald started to panic. He threw open the door.

Franklin grabbed his arm. "Wait! You mustn't touch the ground and any part of the vehicle at the same time! You must leap completely free!"

Gerald placed both legs to the side of his seat, balancing his toes over the door's rim, then leaped out, landing on the grass and rolling to a stop. Franklin did the same, tangling himself in the hedges. The two men arrived at the front door simultaneously. As they fell inside the house, another bolt struck the lightning rod on the roof.

Gerald lay on the carpet, his clothes soaked, splotches of mud and grass stuck to his face. Franklin knelt near the doorway, looking equally disheveled, panting heavily. Tory and Michalene scrambled out of their bedrooms.

"Dad, what happened?" Tory demanded.

Gerald wasn't quite ready to speak. He lifted his eyes slowly. His gaze met Franklin's. Franklin wondered what he was thinking. Had Gerald also concluded that Franklin was the cause? Gerald shut his eyes and shook his head. He appeared to have dismissed the notion as ridiculous.

Gerald rose to his feet and wandered over to the front window. Tory and Michalene stood behind him as he pulled back the curtain. There sat the Bonneville, enshrouded in a faint blue glow. Both doors were open. Rain soaked the seats. A large, dark scar was etched on the roof—the lightning had burned off the paint, exposing a patch of silver.

Tory couldn't believe it. "Lightning hit the car!"

Another jolt hit the lightning rod. The television blanked.

"It's starting all over again!" cried Michalene. Her head turned. She was looking at Franklin.

Gerald rushed to the phone and lifted the receiver.

"Who are you calling?" asked Tory.

"Your mother," said Gerald. "I'm warning her not to come home. After that, the fire department. Maybe the police. Maybe both."

As her father dialed, Michalene stepped over to where Franklin knelt. He looked up at her. That look in the young girl's eyes. Franklin knew that she knew.

"We gotta talk," said Michalene. "In private."

. . .

The fire department declined Gerald Mickelson's invitation to come and observe the phenomenon for themselves, advising him to speak with his insurance company about the damage to the car, and requesting that he call again if an actual blaze erupted. After the dispatcher hung up the phone, everyone at the firehouse enjoyed a good laugh.

The police agreed to drive over and take a look. One particular pair of officers happened to be searching for an excuse to park and eat dinner anyway. By the time they arrived, an hour and forty-five minutes later, the force of the storm had waned. Most of the lightning and thunder had moved east. Gerald refused to step out of the house as the officers examined the scorch on the car's roof. He preferred to call out to them from well inside the doorway. The officers parked across the street for a few minutes to see if they might witness a strike on the Mickelsons' lightning rod. According to Mr. Mickelson, his house had been hit thirteen times since 3:30 that afternoon. One officer thought he saw strike number fourteen, but his partner, busily devouring a sub sandwich, missed it. Whatever the case, the police had no precedents for cases involving harassment from lightning bolts. As the storm moved west, the officers finally drove away. They left with an interesting anecdote to tell their families, but other than hinting that Gerald might call the Channel 9 weatherman or Robert Stack from *Unsolved Mysteries,* they left no advice.

Earlier that afternoon, Michalene cornered Franklin inside her room. Franklin tried to evade an immediate discussion of the subject on her mind by noting the three chess games set up on a table along the right wall.

"I see you're a chess player," said Franklin.

Michalene watched his eyes. "Uh-huh. I play by mail."

Franklin read the names on the strips of tape beside each board. *B. Dovzhenko, Kiev, Russia; Y. Chongju, Chinhae, South Korea; J. Chambers, Swan Hill, Victoria, Australia.*

"Your matches are quite international." Franklin pointed to one of the boards. "This fellow from Australia is giving you some real problems. In three moves he will have checkmate. He will sacrifice his rook and then move his knight here. See?"

"Uh-huh." Michalene hesitated, then asked, "So is Benjamin Franklin also an expert on chess?" She watched for his reaction.

137

Franklin did not even skip a beat. "I have heard that he enjoyed the game very much."

Michalene swallowed hard. He would force her to ask the question directly. "Are you . . . are you him?"

"Who?" he asked.

Michalene's voice was barely audible. "Benjamin Franklin."

"Benjamin Franklin?" Franklin laughed. "My dear, sweet Michalene, what a silly question! Ben Franklin died over two hundred years ago. How could I possibly be Benjamin Franklin?"

Michalene's shoulders drooped. She could feel the blood rush into her face.

Just then another jolt of lightning struck the lightning rod. The lamp flickered. She glanced at the lamp, then squarely back at Franklin.

"But . . . " He sat himself in the chair before her desk. "Just for conversation's sake, perhaps we could discuss the question hypothetically."

Michalene caught her breath.

"What if you were to discover that I actually am Benjamin Franklin? What would you do with this scrap of information?"

Michalene could hear her heart pounding. She was hyperventilating. She had been so caught up in the game of proving her theory, she hadn't quite prepared herself for the moment of truth.

"I'd . . . I . . . I don't know."

Franklin picked up the little stuffed Care Bear from the corner of Michalene's desk and pretended to examine it. "Let us suppose that such a person as Franklin had, in fact, breached a porthole to another century, and in the process had shed five full decades of wrinkles and decay. Would you seek to publicize such information? Or could you be entrusted with this secret until such time as Mr. Franklin thought appropriate?"

Michalene suddenly felt intensely frightened, as if staring into the face of a ghost. "Then it's true. You *are* him."

Franklin scoffed. "Don't be ridiculous, my child. How did you conjure such a notion? But speaking hypothetically: *Could you be trusted?*"

She nodded hesitantly, then said with firmness, "Yes. I could be trusted. Cross my heart and hope to die."

Franklin smiled warmly. He stood and walked over to her window. As he gazed out at the continuing storm, his expression grew pensive.

"Oh, no, Michalene. You're much too young to hope for such a thing. I know what it's like to hope to die. Without a doubt, this should have been my fate four days ago. Do you believe in the East Indian notion of reincarnation?"

"No." Michalene was still finding it difficult to breathe. "At least . . . not before today."

"Neither do I," said Franklin. "Not in the Oriental sense, anyway. But in the realm of natural philosophy, I have come to believe that all things are possible. I have been given an opportunity that perhaps no other human being has received since the dawn of time—to live again. To rechart the course of destiny. To etch into my little book of virtues a whole new list of objectives and ambitions. Your century has so much to offer, Michalene. I do not know where to begin. The possibilities seem infinite. Time has become a more valuable commodity than I had ever previously conceived. Each moment is like an undiscovered nugget of gold. I will not, if I can help it, miss one single excavation. I want to visit every remote corner of our vast and wonderful world and glean its every secret. I think I would like to fly in one of those rocket ships that shoots flames out of its tail. I would like to visit the moon and then I would like to see the stars. Can I do such things? I will not listen if you say that I can't."

Michalene nodded. "If you want it bad enough, they say you can do anything." She was dizzy. She had to sit down. She found a place on the bed.

"I have striven for eighty-four years to achieve perfection," Franklin continued. "I'm afraid I fell far short of it, though I know I was a better and happier man for having made the attempt. This time around, I might actually attain it. I wish I still had my little book. I'll purchase another and record my progress. But before I can begin this quest, there is something I must do. Actually, I should not doubt that in the doing, my quest will have already begun. But to accomplish this thing, Michalene, I will need your help most desperately."

Michalene felt drained. Her mind continued spinning. The last thing she wanted to do was run an errand or burden herself with more obligations. Despite her exhaustion, despite her fear, she responded to the request of Benjamin Franklin with positive fidelity. "What will we try to do?"

Franklin turned to her. His eyes were deadly serious. "We will attempt to save the life of a future candidate for the presidency of the United States."

Michalene raised her eyebrows. "Future president? Who's that?"

"None other than your brother, Torrence Mickelson."

CHAPTER 11

If Franklin had not had such a serious expression, she might have burst out laughing. Tory for president? Could there exist a more ludicrous image? The Tory she knew could barely muster the ambition to read a comic book, let alone run for the most ambitious office in the country. Anyway, how could Ben Franklin know that Tory would one day run for president?

Michalene was having enough trouble swallowing this whole situation as it stood. Why did he have to compound the confusion by uttering such a silly thing? She relived all her old doubts. This wasn't Benjamin Franklin at all. Just some nut case like she'd first thought—some hack actor so intoxicated with his role that he'd forgotten the difference between fantasy and reality. And she'd played right into his hands! How could she have been so gullible?

One last time Michalene rehearsed in her mind all of her far-out reasons for concluding that this man was Benjamin Franklin: things he knew, things he said, things that were happening. There was no other explanation! It *had* to be him! It *was* him! No more games. She needed to hear it from the horse's mouth.

Franklin must have read her mind, because at that moment he pulled up a chair, sat directly in front of her, and took her hand. "Yes, Michalene. You need not doubt any further. I am Benjamin Franklin."

Michalene opened her mouth to speak. Her lips tried to form a question, but nothing came out. She had been many things in her life, but she had never been speechless.

"I know you must have many questions," said Franklin. "I'll do my best to explain everything to you. This matter must be tremendously difficult to comprehend. It's the same for me, I assure you. I will tell you what I know. Beyond that, I would be very interested in hearing your own speculations. You're a clever girl, Michalene. I shall not underestimate your insights."

Franklin told her about the rejuvenation chamber. He told her how the chamber had done more than restore his youth; it had sent him on an odyssey through time. He explained how he had seen events from both the past and the future before settling into the present. He told her about the political rally in the year 2020 and he revealed the details of Tory's death in the churning waters below the spillway.

Michalene looked confused. The same question that had haunted Franklin now popped into *her* mind: How could both visions be true?

"I've come to realize more profoundly than ever before," said Franklin, "that the future is what we make of it. It is not set in stone. It's up to us to make certain that Tory does not drown in that river."

"But how can we stop it?" Michalene wondered. "What could we do?"

"I'm not quite sure," Franklin replied. "That's why I need your help."

"When is this supposed to happen? For all we know, it might not happen for months. We could wait years!"

Franklin shook his head. "If my instincts are intact

enough to judge anything, this event will take place very soon. A matter of days, I should think."

"Then one of us should stay with him at every moment," said Michalene.

"That will be easy," said Franklin, "until Tory decides otherwise. Keeping an eye on a thirteen-year-old who does not wish to be watched is virtually impossible. I apprehend that the most important question is not *when* Tory will crawl out on that pipe, but *why*."

"Why? How could we ever know for sure?"

"I was rather hoping that *you* might shed some light on this."

"Me?" said Michalene. "It wouldn't surprise me if Tory crawled out on that pipe for no reason at all. Just goofing around and taking things too far."

Franklin nodded thoughtfully. "Then we must help your brother to comprehend his own mortality."

"What if he's trying to commit suicide?" asked Michalene.

"Then we must teach him the difference between those things we can change and those things we cannot."

"What if somebody *forces* him to crawl out there?" asked Michalene.

"Then he must learn that for every choice, there is a consequence. Rarely is evil inflicted without cause. Generally, we can account for it by our own unwise decisions well beforehand."

"This is crazy!" shouted Michalene. "How are we gonna teach him all this stuff in just a few days? I'm not sure I understand what you're talking about myself."

"It is a challenge," Franklin confessed. "I suggest we begin with the items most predominant in Tory's life. We must search within these issues and events to see if we might discover where potential powder kegs are concealed."

Michalene remembered something significant. "Giles Peck! My brother is meeting with Giles Peck and his gang of mega-creeps tomorrow night. If ever there was an unwise choice—!"

"Excellent!" said Franklin. "In place of this meeting, we must give him a better option."

"I got a better idea," said Michalene. "Let's just lock him in a closet."

"That might work," said Franklin, "if we could be reasonably assured that he would never get out again for the rest of his life. As well might one halt the course of a great river with his puny arm as try to change the nature of man by compulsion."

Michalene scrutinized Franklin suspiciously. "Do you make up all these sayings as you go along?"

Franklin smiled. "Only the cleverest ones. For the rest, I must happily credit someone else."

. . .

As the evening wore on, the storm calmed, as did the general mood in the Mickelson home. The rain stopped; Gerald called Bonnie to tell her it was safe to come home. She arrived sometime after 7:00 and immediately sequestered herself in her bedroom to type out the details of the various lightning attacks. With any luck, she would see it published on the front page of the *Elysia Gazette.*

Franklin and the children spent the evening watching television. Someone popped *The Wizard of Oz* into the VCR. Michalene remained in the love seat across the room. She had seen the movie at least eight times. This time, she felt not so inclined to watch Dorothy dance with the Scarecrow as to watch the faces of Benjamin Franklin and her brother. The revelations she had received this day about the identity and destiny of these two people were too much to digest.

At every lull Tory would beg Franklin to turn off the movie and play him a game of Nintendo. For a thirteen-year-old boy, watching such a movie was not an especially cool way to spend an evening. Franklin, however, sat mesmerized by the film and declined Tory's invitations. After all, he might relate to Dorothy Gale's predicament more easily than anyone else in the world.

Michalene watched her brother catch a fly in his fist and proceed to pull off its wings. The question again repeated in her mind: Tory Mickelson for president? She still could not believe it. Maybe what Franklin had seen was all part of a joke, like *Pat Paulsen for President,* or *Picard/Riker '92.*

Then there was Benjamin Franklin. Michalene still had moments of doubt that it was actually him, but those moments were becoming less frequent. It was just so hard to accept that one of the greatest minds in history could be sitting in her living room watching *The Wizard of Oz.* Everything about him was just so *normal.* He itched, he coughed, he complained about having consumed too many Cool Ranch Doritos. When Glenda told Dorothy to click her heels three times and utter "there's no place like home," Ben Franklin even cried. Did all great men and women do such things? It was all so strange to Michalene. There might be great people around her all the time and she would have no way of knowing.

The hardest challenge for Michalene was keeping all of this a secret. If Peter Jennings or Tom Brokaw ever found out that Ben Franklin was in town, her family would become worldwide celebrities overnight. People would suddenly want to know Michalene Mickelson—know her and talk to her. Boys would climb all over each other just to get her autograph.

Please, Mr. Franklin, thought Michalene. *Don't make me keep this a secret for long.* She would help him in every way she could: to save Tory's life, to survive in the twentieth century—anything he asked. But when they were finished, she hoped he might also help her to end her loneliness, fulfill her dreams, and finally become, in the eyes of all the world, someone important.

• • •

Franklin enjoyed a very restful sleep that night. Almost too restful. At no time after closing his eyes did he awaken. He did not recall a single dream. It might as well have been the sleep of the dead. Especially considering the condition of his body when he awakened.

Michalene was the first to discover him on his couch. She was a little surprised. On each of the two previous mornings, Franklin had been the first one up. Yesterday he'd even set the milk and all the bowls and cereals on the table.

"Mr. Franklin?" said Michalene softly.

She leaned a bit closer. She was alarmed to see that his eyes were open. "Are you all right?" she inquired.

"I appear to be somewhat incapacitated," Franklin said with perfect matter-of-factness.

"What do you mean?" Michalene demanded.

"At the moment, I can't move any of my limbs." He made an attempt. His arm came barely an inch off the cushion, then dropped back into place.

Michalene started to panic. "Well, how—? Wha—? How did this happen? What can I do?"

"Come around to my side," Franklin directed.

She walked around to the front of the couch.

"Lift my arm for me," Franklin requested.

Michalene was trembling. She took his arm and raised it up. He winced in pain. She lowered it down.

"No, no," said Franklin. "You're doing splendidly. Raise it up again. Higher."

Michalene followed Franklin's instructions. She repeatedly raised and lowered each arm and leg, as if working the rust out of a piece of machinery. The process continued another fifteen minutes. As Michalene was helping Franklin to sit up on the couch, Mrs. Mickelson entered the living room. Bonnie became alarmed.

"What's the matter, Frank?" Bonnie asked. "Are you sick?"

"His muscles are just really stiff," said Michalene. "We've made a lot of progress but—earlier he couldn't even sit up."

Bonnie looked even more distressed. "What caused this, Frank? Has this ever happened before?"

"I shouldn't be too alarmed," said Franklin. "In a few moments, I expect to be perfectly limber. It does, however, seem to require a bit more effort than yesterday."

"*Yesterday?*" Bonnie cried. "Frank, you should see a doctor about this. It could be something serious."

Michalene nodded. "Good idea, Mom."

"That may be sound advice," said Franklin. "But I have my doubts as to whether a doctor would be of assistance."

"Of course he would," said Bonnie. "I've never heard of a disease where you go to bed perfectly fine and wake up every morning practically paralyzed."

"You don't look good either," added Michalene.

"I don't?"

"No, you don't," said Bonnie. "You look . . . haggard."

"Well," said Franklin, "if you wish to send for a physician, I will not hide in the woodshed."

Bonnie began dialing the phone. "I'll see if Dr. Strong can get you in."

Franklin turned to Michalene. "Won't the doctor come here?"

Michalene shook her head. "We'll have to go to him."

"How unusual. What if I were too ill to get there?"

"Then they'd send an ambulance," she explained. "Like the one you saw the other night."

"What a dreadful waste," Franklin observed. "I'm all for hospitals, but only when care in one's own home cannot be adequately provided. Have doctors grown so rich and indolent that the sick must hobble to them rather than have the doctors seek out the sick?"

Michalene shrugged. "It's just how it is nowadays."

After another moment, Franklin was able to stand. By the time Bonnie got off the phone, he had worked out most of the inflexibility by pacing back and forth across the living room.

"Dr. Strong has a slot at 10:45," Bonnie announced. "I'll take an early lunch and drive you there."

• • •

Franklin was convinced it was some kind of conspiracy.

He sat in Dr. Strong's waiting room with Bonnie, three sniffling children, their parents, and two other persons whose illness Franklin could only imagine. Even in the eighteenth century, when professional medicine remained a combination of science, alchemy, and quackery, Franklin had astutely observed that diseases like colds and consumption were contracted not by mere exposure to cool air or dampness, but by contagion when unaffected persons were made to sit in close quarters with affected persons, thus forcing them to breathe in each other's transpiration. The practice of making sick people sit together in a tiny room for an extended period of time while awaiting treatment was either sheer lunacy or a blatant attempt by a doctor to drum up more business.

Michalene had remained at home. She told Franklin she would try to talk Tory out of meeting with Giles Peck that night. Franklin was anxious to get this doctor business over with. What conclusions could a doctor possibly draw? It was obvious to him that his body was still adjusting to its rejuvenation. He might experience these kinds of physical inconveniences and modifications for months, maybe years.

Bonnie filled out the necessary paperwork on Frank Benjamin, agreeing to pay the fifty-five dollar office charge out of her own pocket. For an address she gave her own. As to whether he had any allergies to medications, Franklin replied that he did not know of any. As to his prior medical history, he reported that he had, in the past, suffered from the gout, but he apprehended that such sufferings had ended.

It was 11:30 before the nurse finally invited him to come into the back part of the clinic. She weighed him, then led him into an even smaller room where she took his pulse and temperature.

As she applied the blood-pressure cuff, Franklin exclaimed, "Sphygmomanometer! I am already acquainted with this device. I'll wager a Dutch dollar it will say I am 120 over 80."

"You owe me a Dutch dollar," said the nurse. "You're 130 over 96."

Franklin was a bit taken back. "Is that good?"

"It's a little high."

"Are such things so apt to change in the course of two days?"

"Possibly. You'll have to ask the doctor."

She left. Ten more minutes passed. Franklin sat alone in the sterile silence. He wished he'd brought his magazine with him. Before the nurse had called for him, he'd been reading an intriguing article on virtual reality.

At last Dr. Strong arrived. Franklin was pleasantly surprised to see that the man was a neatly groomed Negro. He appeared to be in somewhat of a hurry. The doctor paid him a brief sideways glance, but for the most part kept his eyes on the paperwork in his clipboard.

"Okay," he intoned. "Mr. Benjamin, I'm Dr. Strong. Have you been waiting long?" The question sounded like a standard icebreaker.

"I'm no worse for wear," said Franklin. "I presume you are a very busy man. And I must say, it is refreshing to see how far your people have come."

Dr. Strong looked up. "My 'people'?"

"Yes," said Franklin. "You are proof of what I have always purported: the Negro mind, when given the advantage of a proper education, is not in the least deficient in natural understanding."

"Glad to be of service in proving your theory." The doctor sounded a bit sarcastic. Franklin ignored it.

"That's quite all right. To my detriment, I have only trumpeted such views in recent years. Since my conversion, however, my support for abolitionist causes has been unyielding."

"Thank you," said Dr. Strong. "But I'm doing just fine."

At last Franklin realized he had offended the man. "Of course you are. I didn't mean to imply—"

"Listen, Mr. Benjamin. I'm black. I'm a doctor. Deal with it."

Franklin felt deeply embarrassed. Apparently, the maverick attitudes he had espoused in his day had grown somewhat archaic. Dr. Strong wanted to be seen by him merely as a fellow human being. For a one-time slave-owner like Benjamin Franklin, it was a modest leap.

"Now what seems to be the problem?" Dr. Strong continued.

"I seem to have a slight case of morning paralysis," said Franklin.

"Paralysis? What do you mean?"

"A stiffness in my joints. But I do not think there's any cause for worry. At the moment I feel perfectly fine."

"You say you have this condition just when you wake up in the morning?"

"For the last three mornings," Franklin clarified. "Each morning the stiffness appears to be somewhat more acute than the last."

Dr. Strong noted the information on the chart. "It says here you've suffered from gout in the past. Is that what this feels like?"

"Not at all. This particular condition is attended much more by immobility than pain."

"Well, this doesn't sound like anything I'm familiar with," said the doctor.

Franklin might have guessed as much. Undoubtedly the ill effects of time travel were as yet undiagnosed by the medical world. As well might one know how to treat seasickness on a globe without oceans.

The doctor reached into a cabinet. "Let's take some blood and urine."

"Urine?"

He handed Franklin a small plastic container. "I'll have you fill this in a minute."

"And what is to be learned by this?"

"Sometimes we can find toxins. We won't know till we run the tests. When was your last tetanus shot?"

"Tetanus shot? Is that a type of inoculation?"

"Uh, yes."

"Then I do not recall that I have ever had one."

"Have you had any recent scrapes or cuts on metal?"

"No."

"Have you recently traveled out of the country?"

"Not specifically."

Dr. Strong raised his eyebrows to request clarification.

"Not for six years," said Franklin.

"Give me your hand," said Dr. Strong. "This won't hurt a bit."

He pricked Franklin's finger and pressed the blood onto a small plastic square.

The doctor continued. "Has anything like this ever happened to anyone in your family?"

"Not that I recall," said Franklin.

"Have you taken any drugs recently? Prescription or recreation?"

"Recreation?"

"Illegal substances," the doctor said wearily.

"Contraband? Oh, no. Just my gout medicine. Laudanum, mixed with a small glass of Madeira."

"Laudanum?" His eyes widened. "You mean opium?"

"Why, yes."

The doctor looked astonished. "You took opium for gout? A doctor *prescribed* this?"

"Yes. My own family doctor. Dr. Jones is a very able man, although compared to yourself his methods may seem outmoded."

"Outmoded? Who do you take me for, Mr. Benjamin? Is this Dr. Jones a licensed practitioner?"

"Is a license now required in this country? Well, I heartily approve."

Dr. Strong was almost beside himself. "Your doctor should be in prison! Mr. Benjamin, haven't you ever heard of Allopurinol?"

"I'm afraid not. I don't know that such a substance was available when—"

"Mr. Benjamin, do you know how addictive opium can be?"

"Oh, yes. For two years I was an utter slave to it. Recent events, however, seem to have cleansed my constitution of such dependence."

"How long have you been off it?"

If Franklin had answered according to his own perceptions, he would have said six days. But he felt such an answer might be misleading, considering all that had happened.

"Quite some time," he replied.

Dr. Strong shook his head. "I've never heard of this kind of delayed side effect with opium. Or any other drug for that matter. Hopefully, we'll learn something from the lab. Until then I'm going to prescribe an anti-inflammatory for the stiffness in your joints. Take it three times a day, with meals."

"You're very gracious," said Franklin.

"I have one more question for you, Mr. Benjamin." Dr. Strong hesitated. "Do you have any history of mental illness?"

It was Franklin's turn to be offended. "Sir, are you implying that I am not in possession of my faculties? That my condition is an aberration of the mind? Absolutely not."

The doctor nodded, unconvinced. He placed Franklin's paperwork on the table beside him and began to fill out the prescription. As he glanced at the information on the chart, he noted Franklin's age.

"It says here you're thirty-two. Is that a typo, or is that when you stopped counting?"

Franklin was confused. "Pardon me?"

Dr. Strong turned around and faced Franklin. "Well, now, Mr. Benjamin. If you're only thirty-two years old, I must be twenty-one."

What was he talking about? Franklin had seen himself in the mirror only last night.

"And how old would you say I am?" asked Franklin.

"Oh, forty-five. Forty-six. Am I close?"

Franklin nodded reservedly. "Yes . . . yes, very close. Is there a mirror in your bathroom?"

"I believe so." He indicated the container in Franklin's hand and pointed out the bathroom door across the hall. "Fill it, if you would, and then give it to the nurse. Have a good day, Mr. Benjamin."

Anxiously, Franklin slipped inside the bathroom. Before gazing into the mirror, he closed his eyes to try to recall the image he had seen of his own face the night before. By recalling this image, he could draw comparisons. Franklin opened his eyes and put his nose up to the mirror.

What the doctor had said was true. The furrows in his brow. The sags under his eyes. The quality of his skin. The grayness at his temples. Franklin felt the grooves on his forehead and pressed back his bangs. When he looked at his hand, it was covered with hair. He was shedding like a horse! Franklin had aged. He had aged dramatically! At least fourteen years in one night! A tremor of fear gripped him. With the lid still down, he sat on the toilet. He let the plastic urine container drop from his hand and roll around in the sink.

His eyes went blank. His breathing quickened. He tried

desperately to grasp the meaning of this. Fifteen years in one night. How was it possible?

Am I dying?

All his renewed hopes and visions, his resurrected dreams of a brighter future, his plans to explore the globe, achieve perfection, and visit the stars—all of this had crumbled in a matter of seconds. It had all been a cruel illusion! The chamber had not bought him a second life. It had only bought him a couple of days—maybe a week.

And then Franklin recalled Scat the cat—his first object of success in achieving rejuvenation in a living thing. As he recalled, the cat's rejuvenation was only fleeting. In seven days, Scat was dead. He had thought he'd resolved this defect. He knew now that he had not. For a brief instant Franklin contemplated mercifully ending his own life.

I will not watch myself crumble and decay again. No man should have to witness such an event twice.

There was only one thought that stopped him. The life of a boy. A boy he had known only three days. If it meant that he could save this one boy and make it possible for him to fulfill his destiny, it would have been worth it.

But this wasn't the only reason. Franklin could not deny there were many reasons it had all been worth it. Everything he had seen. Everything he had learned. What man on the brink of death would not have given his last farthing for a chance to live one week in the distant future and witness for himself the effects of his life's work and the current state of humanity?

It had been a glorious blessing! *Glorious!* Franklin had no cause for regret.

This last mission—to save Tory Mickelson—would now consume his every thought, his every action. It was a race against time. How could he possibly succeed? At best, he

155

had only a few short days. Who knew how his health might deteriorate? Within hours he might become incapable of helping anyone. Was it futile to try to save this boy? With grave apprehension, Franklin performed the necessary math in his mind.

If he could expect the same rate of decay tomorrow as today, by morning he would be sixty. By Sunday, seventy-four. By Monday, eighty-eight. By Tuesday, one hundred and four! And by Wednesday, without a doubt . . .

Benjamin Franklin would be dead.

CHAPTER 12

The doctor thought it might be five or six days before he got the reports back from the lab. Franklin wasn't particularly curious to learn what the reports had to say since he knew he wouldn't be around to benefit.

Bonnie drove him to the nearest pharmacy to fill his prescription for 800 milligrams of Ibuprofen. The line was long. While waiting, Franklin was given ample opportunity to read the labels on the myriad of over-the-counter drugs for sale. He shook his head. He had never thought it wise for a person to indulge too much in medication, convinced that its liberal use impaired the body's natural ability to heal itself. In his own life he had taken pharmaceuticals only as a last resort. After receiving the Ibuprofen, Franklin stuck the bottle in his pocket and forgot it.

Bonnie dropped him off at the house. She insisted that he postpone his yard work for at least a few days, until it could be determined that he was getting better instead of worse. Franklin reminded her that he felt perfectly fine. There was no cause for worry.

As Franklin watched Bonnie drive away, he knew she was unconvinced. The physical difference between the Franklin of last night and the Franklin of this morning was too significant. Mrs. Mickelson knew he was very sick. No doubt Tory and Gerald would believe the same as soon as they got a good look at him. By tomorrow, his accelerated aging would be impossible to deny. He'd be forced to confess his identity to every member of the family. If he failed to tell them everything, they might feel obligated to commit him to some kind of medical facility. Such a decision could prove fatal for Tory.

As Franklin approached the house he was greeted by the worried face of Michalene. Seeing him in the sunlight, she was further convinced that something was seriously wrong. And yet he was smiling and cheerful. There was no sign at all of the crippling stiffness that had stricken him this morning. Except for looking like he hadn't slept in weeks (maybe months!) there was no sign of illness at all.

"What did the doctor say?" asked Michalene.

Franklin was circuitous. He did not feel the moment was right to disclose his impending deterioration. "He gave me a few pills, declared me fit as an ox, and sent me on my way."

Michalene appeared doubtful. "He did? But you look so *tired.*"

"But I feel marvelous!" To prove it Franklin leaped up and clicked his heels.

Michalene smiled. She was deeply relieved.

Franklin put his arm around her and led her inside. "And now"—he glanced around to be sure that Tory was not about—"how goes our plan to dissuade your brother from meeting with this gang of ruffians?"

"Excellent," said Michalene. "Tonight we're all going to the carnival."

• • •

At first Tory seriously objected to the idea of accompanying Franklin and Michalene to the annual summer carnival. But it wasn't because he recalled having an important

158

meeting with Giles Peck; it was because he was flat broke. Grudgingly, Michalene agreed to meet all his expenses.

Tory almost fainted. "Did you just say you were gonna pay my way, or have I died and gone to heaven?"

Michalene wanted to retort, "I'm paying your way to try to *keep* you from dying and going to heaven." Instead, she forced a smile and said, "You bet."

On his fingers, Tory cheerfully reminded her of each projected expense: An all-day ride pass was $12, food might add up to $10, games would undoubtedly come to $10 or $15 . . .

Michalene nodded and gritted her teeth. She'd *better* be saving his life; otherwise she was sorely tempted to kill him.

The carnival would remain open until midnight. Surely the meeting with Giles had been scheduled for earlier. Michalene figured if she and Franklin could keep Tory entertained until closing, their mission would be accomplished.

Franklin and the children spent much of the afternoon huddled around a game of Risk. The first game ended abruptly, partly because Franklin, having been taught the rules but not the stratagems, was easily defeated; partly because Tory, after Michalene had breached his strongholds in Asia and Australia, tossed the entire game into the air, causing a shower of plastic pieces.

Tory demanded a rematch. This time Michalene was the first player out of the game. Franklin had caught the knack of it and at one point held the continents of North America, South America, and Africa. Once again Tory seemed destined to lose, but on his next turn, Franklin placed his armies very sloppily, allowing Tory to breach both Africa and North America. Within three turns the game was over. Tory was victorious.

As her brother bounced around the house in a victory

dance, Michalene whispered to Franklin accusingly, "You let him win, didn't you?"

"Know the worth of your wars," said Franklin. "By conceding a trifling defeat, I might win the greater victory."

And in fact, Michalene was amazed to see that Tory was perfectly attentive when Franklin invited him over to the kitchen table to show him how to make magic squares. Considering that Tory had flunked just about every math course he'd ever taken, this was quite an accomplishment. On a piece of paper Franklin drew a square with eight lines across and eight lines down. After recalling the proper sequences and arrangements, he drew a number in each of the sixty-four boxes.

52	61	4	13	20	29	36	45
14	3	62	51	46	35	30	19
53	60	5	12	21	28	37	44
11	6	59	54	43	38	27	22
55	58	7	10	23	26	39	42
9	8	57	56	41	40	25	24
50	63	2	15	18	31	34	47
16	1	64	49	48	33	32	17

"Now, pay attention," said Franklin. "By employing simple addition, you will discover that each straight row—horizontal or vertical—makes 260. As well, any half row added with another half row equals 260. Any bent diagonal row of eight numbers, such as 16 up to 10 and 23 down to 17, will make 260. Any diagonal row parallel to this bent diagonal row, such as from 50 up to 54 and 43 down to 47, or 9 up to 12 and 21 down to 24, will equal 260. Also, the three diagonal numbers at the corners, such as 53 up to 4 and

29 down to 44, when added together with the two numbers in each corresponding corner, will make 260. As well, each diagonal row of two numbers at the corners, such as 14 up to 61, 36 down to 19, and the lower four numbers situated likewise, will make 260. Lastly, each of the four corner numbers, added to the four numbers in the center, will equal 260."

"Totally cool!" said Tory.

"Yes, totally," Franklin agreed.

"Did you invent this?"

"I did."

"With a computer?"

"Only the springs and gears in my head. I did the same with a box four times as large, but I'll spare you the monotonous details."

"When did you have time to make this up?" asked Michalene.

Franklin leaned toward her ear. "Some sessions of the Pennsylvania Assembly were duller than others."

"So what makes it work?" asked Tory.

"Plain logic," Franklin replied. "If you study it, you will soon discover the pattern. The same mathematical logic may be used to resolve virtually any matter that might vex you."

"What do you mean?" asked Tory.

Franklin went on to describe his system of Moral Algebra. When in life difficult decisions presented themselves, he instructed the children to take a sheet of paper, make two columns, and label them *Pro* and *Con*. Over the course of several days' consideration, they were to write under each column every reason that came to mind for or against a particular measure. Afterwards, they would estimate a respective numerical value for each of the reasons. When there were two, one on each side, that seemed equal, he told them to strike them both out. If one reason *Pro* equaled two reasons *Con,* they should strike out the three, and so forth. In time, Franklin assured them, they would discover where the balance lay and come to a determination accordingly. Though perhaps not as precise as algebraic quantities, Franklin was convinced that such a system had given him great advantage in better judgment throughout his life and had made him considerably less liable to make a rash step.

Michalene noticed that Tory listened in awe. She hoped that some of this was actually penetrating his brain. Michalene marveled at Franklin's uncomplicated wisdom. Such things might be exactly what Tory needed to hear.

"How do you know so much stuff?" Tory asked.

"Stick to my side, my boy," said Franklin. "There are many wonders we shall yet discover together."

Michalene couldn't remember the last time someone had given them so much undivided attention. And then she realized the secret. It wasn't so much what was taught. It was the love of the teacher.

Suddenly Michalene wanted to cry. She wasn't sure why. Perhaps it was gratitude. Who needed a guardian angel? She and Tory had Benjamin Franklin. He would willingly look after them, teach them, and even, if necessary, save them. Perhaps her tears were out of fear. Franklin didn't look good. He didn't look good at all. What would they do if they lost him? Who would save them then?

So that no one would see her crying, Michalene escaped to her bedroom. Nestled in her pillow, she became nostalgic for the days before Franklin had arrived, days when she'd barricaded herself from caring about anyone. It had been better not caring, she thought. If caring about someone meant you had to live in constant fear of losing them, she didn't much like it at all.

• • •

It was a perfect evening for the carnival. To Franklin's relief there weren't more than a few clouds in the sky. Had there been the least indication of inclement weather, he would have been very apprehensive about stepping outside of the house.

It appeared as though the whole town had taken advantage of the clear evening. The carnival was packed. Franklin hadn't witnessed such a gala affair since leaving France. There were hundreds of people flitting to and fro, balloons, cotton candy, games of chance, and thrill rides that more closely resembled mechanical monsters. In fact, many of the rides were named for monsters—the Titan, the Dragon, the Cyclops, the Octopus.

Franklin watched some of the rides run their course and found it hard to believe that people could voluntarily subject their bodies to such abuse. However, when Michalene offered to buy Franklin a ride ticket, he replied with an eager "Yes!"

Michalene was still concerned for his health. "Are you sure you feel up to it?"

"Of course," Franklin replied. "Did you think I wanted to let you children have all the fun?"

After their first bout with a ride called "The Rocket," Franklin decided his initial instincts had been correct. He reported to the children the need for a few moments of recovery before boarding the next ride. That way his stomach might settle back into its natural cavity.

In the meantime, Tory dragged them over to a game

booth whose walls were decorated from floor to ceiling with stuffed *Jurassic Park* dinosaurs.

"A winner every time!" barked the vendor.

Tory turned to Michalene and Franklin. "Let's all three do it," he suggested. "That way, we're *sure* to win."

Michalene gave in. After handing the vendor three dollars, she and Franklin sat themselves in a stool beside Tory and seven other players. The object of the game was to shoot with a water pistol into the mouth of a clown. A balloon would then inflate atop the clown's head. The first balloon to burst determined the winner. Tory was frustrated when a little old man on the end stool won the first round. What did he think he was he going to do with a stuffed triceratops anyway? Even more frustrated was Michalene, who had to shell out three more dollars.

The victor in round two was none other than Benjamin Franklin.

"Number nine! A winner!" announced the vendor, handing Franklin his prize.

Tory stepped over to admire the little stuffed Tyrannosaur. "All right, Frank!" he declared.

Franklin eyed the toy warily. "And what kind of creature is this?"

"A T-Rex," said Tory.

"T-Rex?"

"Short for Tyrannosaurus Rex," said Michalene.

"That sounds Latin." Franklin recalled the translation. "Yes. *Tyrant Lizard King.* Is this an actual animal species?"

"You've never heard of a T-Rex?" said Tory. "Now *that* I find hard to believe."

"And what corner of the globe does this creature inhabit?"

"It's a dinosaur," said Michalene. "They've been extinct for millions of years."

Franklin's eyes widened. *"Millions?"*

Michalene nodded. "Millions. All that we know about them comes from prehistoric fossils dating back to the Triassic, Jurassic, and Cretaceous periods, over sixty-five million years ago."

"Why, that's astonishing!" declared Franklin. He had never conceived that the world could be so old. In his own day, Franklin had occasionally noted certain fossil curiosities, but he'd never heard such detailed conclusions about their origin. He found it ironic that only in the future had men begun to unlock the mysteries of the past. What an age! To have the future and the past so readily at one's fingertips! He couldn't help but wonder: had such knowledge produced in mankind a sense of awe or arrogance? In light of such knowledge, how could men not begin to see themselves above their Maker? Hopefully, humanity had not become so proud in understanding, like some Greeks of old, as to halt its quest for Divine wisdom. At such a juncture, men might continue to gather knowledge, but they would cease to learn truth.

Franklin persuaded the children to ride something a little less jolting. The Ferris wheel was just the remedy. It was actually one of the largest portable models utilized by traveling carnivals, lifting the riders high enough to see all of Elysia and the surrounding county. Before the ride commenced, the chair occupied by Franklin and the children came to rest at the very pinnacle while other riders loaded and unloaded below. The lights of the carnival had started to burn brightly. Franklin gazed off toward the west. The red-orange sunset glinted off the river. This was exactly how

Franklin wished to remember the twentieth century: music, lights, and excitement, all nestled upon a limitless landscape.

Franklin enjoyed the Ferris wheel enormously and would have preferred another ride equally tame, but Michalene had her eye set on the Octopus. En route to this eight-armed contraption, Tory became distracted by the basketball toss.

"Wait!" he cried to the others. "Let's play this!"

"Haven't we spent enough money on games?" protested Michalene.

"But I can win this," said Tory.

The prize for two consecutive baskets was a large model airplane glider. Franklin instantly sympathized. Had he been born in the twentieth century, he was confident that he would have learned how to fly one of these devices as soon as he was old enough to walk.

"Are you certain you can win it?" said Franklin.

"Piece of cake," Tory replied.

Michalene scoffed. "It's a rip-off! The baskets are smaller than normal."

To prove her wrong, the vendor tossed a basketball and split the net.

"See!" said Tory. "Give me five bucks—in case I don't make it the first time."

Michalene grumbled and handed over the money. "I'm not waiting around to watch. We're going to ride the Octopus."

The metallic mollusk was just across the midway. Reluctantly, Franklin let Michalene tow him by the thumb to the ride's gate. They boarded the Octopus right away. The short wait worried Franklin. Obviously few people in their right minds subjected themselves to this particular ride.

"This one is really cool," said Michalene. "As the ride

spins, it almost looks like you're going to ram into another basket, then suddenly you turn."

Thrilling, thought Franklin. Even yesterday, at the age of thirty-two, he might have more readily enjoyed this sort of entertainment. He could still see Tory across the way shooting baskets. The boy made his first shot and missed the other.

As the ride picked up momentum, Franklin experienced a vivid recollection of his time-travel episode. A familiar nausea welled up in his viscera. With any luck, this would be a very brief ride.

On each furious pass, Franklin caught a blurry glimpse of Tory. Once it appeared as though Tory had stopped shooting baskets. He had turned to greet someone. It took a couple more spins before it registered with Franklin that Tory had been joined by a group of boys. Franklin became quite anxious. He knew precisely what group of boys this was.

"Stop the ride!" he cried. "Stop the ride!"

Michalene had also seen the gang surround her brother. She began shouting with Franklin, but with every other spinning rider screaming just as loudly, the men operating the controls ignored them.

"Tory!" Michalene and Franklin cried in unison. "Tory!"

They watched helplessly as Tory followed the boys away from the basketball toss. He and the gang members disappeared into the masses. When the ride stopped, Franklin did not wait for his turn to be unloaded. He leaped from the basket six feet above the ground, earning shouts of anger from the operators. One operator tried to stop him as he rushed out the gate, but Franklin slipped by and pressed his way into the crowd. He scrambled to the end of the carnival midway. Where had Tory gone? There was no sign of him or the other boys anywhere. He dashed back toward the Octopus, hoping he'd passed him in the crowd. On the way back, he met Michalene.

"Did you see him?" she asked frantically.

"I've looked in every direction," said Franklin. "He's nowhere to be seen."

Tory had vanished. Where could he have slipped off to so quickly? Had Tory arranged this rendezvous with the gang of older boys before they left the house? It seemed too great a coincidence that he had met them here by chance. All of their efforts to keep Tory from meeting with Giles Peck and his cronies had failed. For Franklin, the defeat was most bitter. The final objective of his life, on the last day that he may have been healthy enough to do anything about it, appeared hopelessly thwarted.

CHAPTER 13

"I really ought to tell Frank and my sister that I'm goin' off with you guys," said Tory. He followed Giles Peck and the others into the parking lot.

"Don't worry about 'em," said Giles. "We'll have you back before they even notice you're gone."

"What about my bike?" asked Tory.

"What about it?" retorted Giles.

"I left it on the other side. I don't have a very good padlock."

"Listen, kid," said Giles, "if you pull this off for us tonight, I'll buy you a *new* bike."

"My bike *is* new," said Tory.

Giles became a little impatient. "Then I'll buy you whatever you want. Or I'll just give you cash. Does three hundred dollars sound good to you?"

"*Five* hundred dollars sounds better," said Tory.

The other boys laughed. Giles put his arm around Tory's shoulder. "Tory, my man, I like the way your mind works. Five hundred it is. Of course it'll be awhile before I can pay you. It may take me a few weeks to unload the merchandise."

Giles' van was bright orange, decorated with surfers, waves, and bikini-clad beach babes, despite the fact that Giles had never seen an ocean in his life. The other four boys

169

piled into the back. Tory was given the honor of sitting up front with Giles.

"So are we gonna break into Hansen's Market again?" Tory wondered.

Giles shook his head and lit a cigarette. "We're after a little more than beer tonight, kid. We got bigger fish to fry."

As the van pulled onto the street, an argument ensued between the boys in back about how to divide the four remaining cigarettes. Giles told them he didn't care how the smokes were divided as long as Tory got one.

Tory took the Camel graciously, but it was apparent he didn't quite know what to do with it. Smoking was one vice Tory hadn't dabbled in as yet. He stuck the cigarette in his shirt pocket. "I'll save it for later."

"What's the matter, kid?" asked Giles. "Haven't you ever smoked before?"

"Sure, I have," said Tory. "I've just had too many today already."

The boys in back cracked up and jabbed Tory in the shoulder.

Giles scolded the others. "Leave him alone. If Tory wants to wait, he can wait." He winked at Tory. "Stick with me, kid. I'll teach you everything I know. Before long, you'll be running circles around these morons."

The boys in back protested at Giles' insult as much as they dared.

Tory found it curious that Frank Benjamin had made him much the same promise as Giles. Only Frank didn't seem to expect much in return.

Oh, well, thought Tory. *A guy can never have too many friends.*

Tory cracked his window. The smoke was starting to make him nauseous. He noted that Giles drove into one of the poorer neighborhoods in Elysia. A block later, on a street called Shadow Place, Giles turned off the headlights and rolled forward slowly. He coasted to a stop in front of the nicest home in the area. The address was 1001. The house, faintly lit by a nearby streetlight, was almost like a desert oasis—two stories tall, well-groomed lawn, freshly painted. No lights were on. No cars in the driveway.

"Who lives here?" asked Tory.

"The candy man," Giles replied, and the other boys laughed. "He's outa town till tomorrow, which makes things convenient for you."

Tory became nervous. "You want me to break in *there?*"

"No reason to break in," said Giles. "Last night while I was making a social call, I unlatched the bathroom window."

"What do you want me to take?" asked Tory.

"Anything you can find," said Giles. "Down in the basement he's got a lab for making a special kind of vitamin. It has a little cross on the top."

Tory knew what he meant. Whoever lived in that house illegally manufactured speed. It was a methamphetamine lab. Now Tory understood why it was such a nice house in a poor neighborhood: A businessman likes to stay close to his customers.

"You want me to lift all the pills I can find?"

"Now you're catchin' on," said Giles. "I've never been down in the basement, but I've been told he's got a cabinet on the wall. Everything's in there." He reached under his seat and pulled out a crowbar. "He keeps a lock on it. You'll probably need this." Giles groped around in his glove box and found a flashlight. "And this."

Tory looked at the crowbar and flashlight. He shook his head. "I've heard about these kind of places, Giles. When the owner leaves, he rigs them with all kinds of booby traps."

Giles laughed. "You watch too many movies, kid. This'll be like taking candy from a baby. And after I sell the supply, there's five hundred dollars in it for you. I promise."

"I don't want five hundred dollars, Giles. Please. I don't wanna go in there."

"I told you he'd flake," quipped a boy in back.

"Shut up!" Giles snapped at the boy. He spun back to Tory. Giles' expression was now gravely serious. "You're the only one who can fit through that window, Tory. Don't let me down. Not after all the trouble I went through to make sure that window is unlatched. After this, you can hang out with us all the time. We'll always be there for you. For better or for worse. Right, guys?"

"You bet!"

"Absolutely!"

"To the grave, kid!"

Tory was shaking. "I can't do it, Giles. I can't."

Giles let out a long sigh. "All right, Tory. Looks like I'm gonna have to put it to you straight. Either you go into that house, or I'm gonna break every bone in your scrawny little body. Straight enough?"

It seemed that with Giles it was a very short trip from promises of friendship to threats of violence. "Please," Tory begged. "Don't make me do this."

"I don't have time for this, kid." Giles reached out and caught Tory's hand. "I'll start with your fingers—one at a time."

A boy in back pinned Tory's other arm. Giles bent Tory's pinkie as far as it would go before snapping. "Now do you get the picture?"

"No, Giles!" Tory cried. "Okay, I'll do it! I'll go! Don't break it! I'll go!"

Giles released Tory's hand and slapped him on the

shoulder. Once more he was the boy's sincerest friend. "Good man. Sorry to have to get rough. This thing means a lot to us. You okay?"

Tory massaged his hand, looking down at the floor. "Yeah."

"Like I said," Giles continued, "we want you to be one of us. We want it more than anything. But you gotta prove yourself. Think of this as your initiation." Again Giles offered him the crowbar and flashlight.

Tory took them, but he made no move, his gaze lingering on the floor. Giles put his hand under Tory's chin and lifted the boy's face toward the house. He pointed out the bathroom window.

"Right side. Middle window," said Giles. "Use that box on the porch as a boost up. You ready?"

Tory nodded. Giles slapped Tory's knee.

"We'll be waitin' right here for you. Don't stop to watch television. Understand?"

Without responding, Tory climbed out of the van and started across the lawn. Giles and the others watched Tory make his way toward the porch. One boy in back leaned forward to ask Giles a question.

"Was what he said true?" he asked. "Is the house booby trapped?"

Giles shrugged. "How should I know? We're about to find out, aren't we?"

• • •

As instructed, Tory retrieved the plastic crate. As promised, the window was unlatched. He pushed it open and peered into the darkness. Even if he stood on the crate, it would take considerable effort to pull himself up. He wanted to go back to the van and ask for help, but he was reasonably certain that he'd only receive further threats unless he first attempted it on his own.

Tory set the flashlight and crowbar quietly on top of the toilet tank inside the window. He shivered and thought about running—jumping down off the crate and fleeing into the night. But they would find him. Sooner or later, they would find him. He did not doubt Giles' threat. Tory found a grip for each hand along the inside of the windowsill and hoisted himself up.

As he fell inside the house, he injured a rib on the toilet bowl. After pacing the bathroom for a moment, walking off the pain, he flipped on the flashlight. The bulb was awfully dim. Apparently nobody had bothered to check the batteries. The flashlight was barely useful at all. He opened the bathroom door and stepped into the house. The owner was an art nut. Assorted sculptures, modern art stuff with bizarre shapes and twists, adorned the living room. On the walls hung lots of pictures, including Andy Warhol and Salvador Dali, as well as two magazine covers—*Rolling Stone* and *Soldier of Fortune*—blown up and framed. The furniture was leather. The carpet was thick shag.

Tory was convinced he had *not* seen too many movies. Each step was executed with great caution. There were few things a drug dealer despised more than getting ripped off. He'd heard how these guys sometimes booby-trapped the floor with trip wires attached to bombs that would kill the trespasser, but leave the house, for the most part, undamaged.

When he reached the top of the basement stairs, he carefully knelt and shined the light low along the steps, hoping to catch the shine of any wires. The flashlight was too dim. Tory saw a light switch. No harm in turning it on. It would illuminate only the stairway. Nobody outside would see it.

174

But just as he was about to throw the switch, he recalled an old Burt Reynolds movie where someone injected a fluid of some kind into a light bulb. When flipped on, the bulb exploded and the guy became toast. The light bulb was just over his head. It wasn't worth it. He'd brave the steps in the dark.

Each stair creaked softly. But since nothing exploded, Tory safely concluded the stairs hadn't been rigged. At the bottom there was a short landing, and beyond that loomed a door. The hinges opened inward. Tory grabbed the knob, twisted it slowly, and pulled.

He shined the light around the basement. Apparently, he hadn't reached the drug lab part of the house. This room looked like an entertainment area: big screen TV, leather bean-bag chairs, and a CD player with enormous speakers. To his left sat several grocery sacks filled with hundreds of matches. Along the right wall glowed a forty-gallon salt-water aquarium. Bubbles gurgled to the surface. The aquarium light bathed the room in soft blue. Beyond the aquarium, Tory made out a hallway. The lab must be down there. As he stepped into the room, he noticed something else at the end of the hallway. Eyes shining.

Something was *alive* down here! Something with an ominous low growl. The eyes lunged! Tory dropped the flashlight. Unthinking, he also dropped the crowbar, his only possible weapon. He tried to escape back into the stairwell, but he was too late to slam the door behind him. As he started to close it, an enormous pit bull crashed through. Impetuously, the dog started up the stairs. It was halfway to the top before it noticed that Tory was hiding behind the door at the bottom. Before the dog could turn and pounce, Tory spun back into the basement and yanked at the door. The pit bull sprang, slamming against the wood and knocking the door all the way closed. There on the other side, the animal barked and scratched furiously.

Tory sank down on the floor. *Now I've really done it,* he mourned. He was trapped in the basement! Even if he got the drugs, how could he get them out of the house? He collected his wits. There had to be another way out. A basement window—*something!* He wasn't about to face that dog again. He'd dig a tunnel first.

Don't panic, Tory told himself. He found the flashlight and shined it around to locate the crowbar. The dog kept yakking. Tory was in a hurry now. Sooner or later that dog would alert a neighbor. What if someone had been assigned to look after the place while the owner was away? He rushed to the end of the hallway and found another closed door.

When he opened it, there was an ear-rending explosion.

Tory collapsed. He lay there for several moments before regaining his bearings. When he finally came to, he realized he was soaked. For an instant, he thought it was his own blood. But then . . . No. It was only water. In fact, there was a fish flopping beside his hand! Had the fish tank exploded?

Tory sat up. He realized he wasn't badly injured, except for a fierce ringing in his ears. He couldn't hear the dog barking or anything else. What had happened? This was crazy! He had to get out of here! Forget about the drugs! Forget everything!

Tory looked up at the door. There was a hole in it. A hole? Yes, a large hole, the size of a dinner plate, had been blown out of the top half of the door. Tory stood. He shined the flashlight through. It was the drug lab. Propped up at the other side of the room was a shotgun, the barrel still smoking. Somehow the owner of the house had rigged a line from the door handle to the trigger! Had Tory been a mere two inches taller, or standing two inches farther to the right, the buck shot would have taken his head off. It was a small consolation that by rigging this booby trap, the owner had destroyed his own fish tank.

Tory's mind had numbed. If he was terrified, he didn't seem to know it yet. His thoughts raced, yet, paradoxically, his thoughts were clear. He could smell the acrid chemicals. He could see the wall cabinet inside the lab. Tory threw open the door, stepped up to the cabinet, stuck the crowbar into the loop between the hinge and the padlock, and yanked down. The hinge broke. The cabinet fell open. He shined the light inside. All he saw were two cream-colored, misshapen bricks wrapped in cellophane and masking tape. There were no baggies filled with cross-tops. He hoped the find would still be valuable enough to get him off the hook. He wasn't going to look around for anything else.

The ringing in Tory's ears started to subside. The dog was barking as frenetically as ever. He stuffed the off-white bricks under his arm and scrambled toward the other end of the basement. He found a laundry room. Thank goodness! There was a basement window above the washing machine. He climbed on top of the washer. The window had been nailed shut. Tory broke it out with the crowbar. After clearing away as much glass as possible, he climbed into the window well.

Tory found himself in the backyard. With the bricks still under his arm, he made his way around to front of the house. But where was the van? Giles Peck had abandoned him! No doubt they'd heard the dog, then the gunshot, and decided to scram.

It was then that Tory felt the trickle on his ear. He brought up his hand. Blood! The shotgun had not missed entirely. He'd been hit! And only an hour earlier he'd been riding the Ferris wheel at Elysia's summer carnival. Now he was shot in the ear—shot while stealing drugs. The numbness in his emotions had started to thaw, and tears began streaming down his cheeks. He tore off into the night.

Tory ran all ten blocks back to the carnival grounds. The cellophane-wrapped bricks were now tucked under his shirt. He'd expected Giles to drive by him somewhere along the way, but there was no sight of the orange van. As he neared the lights of the carnival, he felt his ear again. Apparently the wound had stopped bleeding. Tory felt relieved. If it wasn't bleeding anymore, it might not be that bad. He wouldn't know for sure until he found a mirror.

Just the same, whenever he ran by people headed home from the carnival, he passed them on the left to hide any evidence of the injury. All he wanted now was to reach his bicycle on the far side of the fairgrounds. Frank and Michalene had locked their bikes to the same tree. Whether or not they'd already left, he was determined to ride home as fast as he could.

Tory made his way around the carnival's perimeter until he reached the tree. As expected, Frank and Michalene had already left, probably searching for him. *No matter,* thought Tory. They'd find him soon enough.

He knelt beside his bike and lined up the three-number combination on the lock. Just as it came loose, he shielded his eyes from a pair of oncoming headlights. The orange van pulled up. Out of the driver's side door emerged Giles Peck.

"Tory! Are you all right? What happened, man? We thought sure you were dead!"

Tory shook his head. "No. But I probably should be."

"Did you get the stuff?"

Reluctantly, Tory pulled the off-white bricks from within his shirt.

"Those aren't pills," Giles observed. "How come—?"

And then he realized what Tory was holding. Giles blurted out a profanity. "Where did you get those?"

"Out of the cabinet," Tory replied. "Just like you said."

Giles laughed in ecstasy. "I don't believe it! You're incredible! Do you know what those are? Do you know how much those are worth?"

Giles stepped forward to relieve Tory of his payload. Before he could take the bricks, a bicycle rolled in between them. Benjamin Franklin stepped off the bike and spoke to Giles.

"I advise you to stand clear of the boy," he directed.

Giles retreated a step, then smiled and asked Tory, "Who's this? Your grandpa?"

"I do not wish to make trouble," said Franklin, "but trouble there will be if you do not get back into your motor coach this instant and ride away."

Giles was now confident he wasn't some kind of cop, nor was he even related to Tory. Except for a girl on another bike about ten yards away, the man was also completely alone.

"No sweat, old man," said Giles. "We were just leavin'. Give me the bricks, Tory."

"I don't expect the boy shall give you anything," said Franklin.

Dismay raced across Tory's features. He'd have preferred to give Giles the bricks and be done with this whole business. Now he'd have to watch Frank get beaten to a bloody pulp.

Giles took a step toward Franklin. The hoodlum's face brightened with recognition.

"I know you now," Giles uttered. "You're that wino!" He turned to other boys, who were now outside the van. "That's him, isn't it? That's the wino we found in the park woods!"

179

"Yeah, you're right," the boys confirmed. "That's him."

Giles turned back to Franklin. "Correct me if I'm wrong, but I thought I told you to stay off our turf."

"You did," Franklin confirmed. "However, I have chosen for the present to disregard such advice."

"Oh, you have?"

"Yes," said Franklin, "until such time as the advice giver can be taught some better manners and a proper respect for his elders."

"I see," said Giles. "And do you intend to teach me these things yourself?"

"Why, I'd be delighted," said Franklin. "But I regret to say that your first lesson might well involve a degree of physical pain."

And with that Franklin assumed the typical stance of an eighteenth-century boxer, with his fists a-twirling before his face. It had been at least fifty years since Franklin's hands had donned any sort of boxing mufflers. He'd have never placed himself in the ranks of such British prizefighting legends as James Figg or Jack Broughton, but he'd once considered himself quite proficient at the sport, proving his deftness on several occasions during his first visit to London. Could such skills ever be entirely forgotten? Since the use of hand mufflers was not nearly as common when Franklin first engaged in the sport, he felt perfectly comfortable with bare fists.

"You gotta be kiddin' me," said Giles.

"I assure you, I am not," Franklin replied.

Franklin might have preferred such a contest yesterday. However, he was only forty-six years old, give or take a year. He seemed to recall several boxers bragging that in their mid-forties they had only just reached their prime.

Giles and his cronies watched Franklin's bizarre display

another few seconds before they all burst out laughing. Franklin maintained a steady smile and a keen eye.

"All right, then," said Giles.

With his companions rooting him on, Giles Peck tore off his shirt and tossed it to the ground. He assumed the stance, not of a boxer, but of a brown belt in Okinawan karate.

Giles made the first lunge—a roundhouse followed by a back kick, but Franklin was not so foolish tonight as that night in the woods. After all, a fighter's first lesson is distance, and since Franklin kept *his,* Giles' kicks met only with the air. When Giles turned again to face his opponent, he met the rapid one-two punch of Benjamin Franklin.

A little more than surprised, Giles staggered back a couple steps and shook himself. He gritted his teeth. "Now you've upset me."

After releasing a high-pitched karate shriek, Giles attempted a second lunge, this one involving a front kick (which missed horribly) and a punch toward the face (which Franklin dodged). Franklin followed up with a double jab to the right eye and a solid punch to the nose. Giles Peck went down.

Now in Franklin's day, it was by no means a standard rule that a fighter could not hit a man while he was down. In fact, to avoid such an opportunity would have been considered foolish. Therefore, as Giles attempted to rise, he met Franklin's fist again, and then once more. Franklin danced around another moment until he realized that Giles was, in fact, out cold.

"Well," said Franklin, "that was a mite easier than I'd anticipated." He turned to the other boys and resumed his fighting posture. "If any more of you young men are in need of instruction, I shall be more than happy to oblige."

The boys looked stunned. Giles had been their leader

primarily because he'd convinced them that he could kick the tar out of any one of them. Come to think of it, except for an occasional assault on a drunk, none of them had ever seen him in an actual fight. His karate moves alone had been intimidating enough. After witnessing Giles' easy defeat, none were particularly eager to take on the old wino again, at least not while he was sober.

The boys stood clear while Franklin took the cellophane-wrapped blocks from Tory and asked him to climb onto his bike. Tory looked up at Franklin in awe.

"You were incredible, Frank," said Tory. "I've never seen anything like that."

Franklin noticed the blood on Tory's shirt. "Are you all right, my boy? Your ear is bleeding."

"I'm fine," Tory insisted.

"I think we should get you home."

Franklin and Tory mounted their bicycles and caught up with Michalene, who had remained the whole time on her own bike ten yards away. She laid into Tory, demanding to know what had happened and how he had cut his ear. A full comprehension of it all had not quite settled over him. He wasn't ready to talk.

"So what are these?" Franklin inquired as they pedaled toward home, referring to the cellophane bricks.

"Two kilos of cocaine . . . I think," Tory replied.

"Cocaine!" Michalene was freaking out.

"And what is cocaine?" asked Franklin.

"Drugs!" Michalene exclaimed. "One of the most illegal and dangerous drugs there is. How could you do this, Tory? You're such an idiot! How did you get involved in all this?"

Tory remained speechless and ashamed.

"There's nothing we can accomplish by heaping further

abuse on the lad," said Franklin. "First we might determine what to do with this contraband."

"I'll show you what we should do with it!" cried Michalene. "Stop your bike!"

The riders had reached one of the bridges overlooking the river. Franklin stopped as Michalene directed. Michalene grabbed the two bricks from him and heaved them out over the railing. The cocaine splashed into the river, promptly sinking to the bottom where Michalene felt sure the stuff could never hurt anybody again.

At last, Tory broke his silence. "I don't know," he told his sister, "if that was such a smart thing to do. In fact, it may turn out to be the stupidest thing you've ever done."

CHAPTER 14

After extracting a sliver from his head near the top of his ear, Tory concluded that his injury had not been caused by buckshot but by flying wood debris as the plate-sized hole exploded out of the door. Covering the wound required only a single Band-Aid. However, this proved to be the least of Tory's physical problems that night.

The sheer stress of Friday's events affected Tory with serious nausea, accompanied by a fever. Michalene didn't understand why her brother had become so ill. Franklin assured her that, like a soldier recovering from battle fatigue, such side effects were quite common. The boy spent much of the night tossing with nightmares and retching into the toilet. Bonnie awakened once to see what was the matter. Michalene explained to her that Tory had gotten ill by eating too much pizza at the carnival. When Bonnie inquired about her son's ear, Michalene told her that some little kids had thrown rocks at them. She was amazed at how easily the lies came into her head. After Bonnie went back into her bedroom, Franklin gave Michalene a disapproving glance.

"Honesty is always the best policy," he told her. "Parents are not always as prone to stark-raving hysterics as the child might think."

"You obviously don't know *my* parents," said Michalene.

"You forget that I *am* a parent," said Franklin. "Of

course, there is always that initial conniption fit, but it will soon pass. Remember, all parents were children once. Their wisdom in resolving complicated matters may even surprise you. I suggest you tell them every detail tomorrow."

Michalene appeased him with a nod and went to bed. When at last it appeared that Tory had fallen asleep, Franklin retired to his own place on the couch. He sat there for some time without laying his head on the pillow. He was utterly exhausted, but he was infinitely more afraid of what might greet him in the mirror when he awakened. Earlier, Franklin had looked himself over in the mirror and decided that he had not aged more than a year since that morning. Sleep accelerated the aging process. By refusing to sleep, could he halt the flow of years?

Franklin scoffed at himself. *Halt the flow of years, indeed.* His thoughts reminded him of a vain young maiden gripping tenaciously to a jar of wrinkle cream. It was in his later years that he had considered himself the most creative and productive. Perhaps he should look *forward* to waking up in the morning. Oh, if not for the pains and ills of the body, Franklin would have confidently reported that old age was actually a preferable thing. Certainly not a condition to be despised. But none of this mattered. His eyes were drooping and his thoughts were drifting.

His dreams commenced even before his head hit the pillow. Only vaguely did he recall lying down. He snapped alert a few minutes later. He could already feel the atrophy taking hold of his muscles. Franklin could stave off sleep no longer. It was as if fourteen years of sleepless nights were dragging at his eyelids. In another moment, the philosopher had fallen hopelessly, irrevocably, into a state of slumber.

• • •

Tory awakened earlier than usual. The nausea had subsided for the most part, but he felt weak and achy. His mouth was dry. Bleary-eyed, the boy ambled out of bed and made his way into the hall. He heard quiet voices in the living room. Someone was crying. Tory edged up to the wall and peeked around the corner.

The tears were Michalene's. He noticed her standing over the couch where Frank slept. Tory could see only the back of the couch. He couldn't see Frank on the cushions. He watched Michalene lift Frank's leg and bend it at the knee. She repeated the action five or six times, then did the same with his other leg. All the while, tears streamed down her cheeks. Tory could hear Frank's voice.

"I'm sorry, my child," Franklin said. "I should have told you yesterday. The aging appears to accelerate when I sleep, adding another thirteen or fourteen years every night."

"How can we stop it?" Michalene asked.

"I'm not certain that we can," said Franklin. "It seems that my physical transformation in the chamber was only temporary. I should be grateful that I do not reawaken each morning in some past decade as I am drawn back to the year 1790. You mustn't weep for me, Michalene. You must be strong."

"How can I be strong when you're dying?" she asked.

"Because I need you to be strong," said Franklin. "There is still much we can do."

She continued to bend Franklin's leg at the knee. "Can you move it by yourself yet?"

Franklin gave it a try. Michalene stood back to watch. From Tory's perspective, he couldn't tell if he succeeded. Any success must have been limited. Michalene started lifting the leg and bending it again.

"We have to get you walking before my parents wake up," Michalene whispered.

"You can't hide me away like a pair of stockings," said Franklin. "We will have to tell them who I am."

"Are you kidding? I tried to tell Tory who you were and he thought I'd gone bonkers."

"When they see me, they will know."

"They're not *gonna* see you," said Michalene. "If they see you, they'll have people come and take you away. Now try again. Move your leg. You have to help me."

Tory could resist his curiosity no longer. He crept out from around the corner and approached the couch. When Michalene saw him, she gasped. Tory did not falter. He continued forward until he could see Franklin's face. The boy tried not to show any expression at all, but his hands were quivering.

The man on the couch was close to sixty years old. His hair was thin. The wrinkles in his brow had deepened. There was no denying it now. This person was an exact duplicate of the man pictured on the one hundred dollar bill.

Franklin looked concerned at first, then a warm smile came to his face. "Good morning, Torrence."

Tory's eyes thinned. "Who *are* you?"

Franklin glanced at Michalene. Surely Tory had overheard them. It was useless to keep him from the truth.

"My name is Benjamin Franklin."

Tory's expression did not change, but his hands continued to shake. "Why did you come here? What do you want from us?"

"I want nothing from you," said Franklin. "Only your friendship. I assure you, my arrival here was strictly by chance."

"*How* did you come here?" asked Tory.

187

"Through time, young man. I came here through the medium of time."

"How come you're getting so old?"

"I wish I could answer that," said Franklin. "I was old when I left. My body seems to be reverting back to its original condition."

"How old were you when you left?" asked Michalene.

"I was eighty-four."

"So when you reach eighty-four," Michalene wondered, "will you stop aging?"

"Perhaps," Franklin speculated. "But I'm not confident this will make any difference. I was only hours away from my own death when I entered my rejuvenation chamber."

"Rejuvenation chamber?" repeated Tory. "Is that some kind of time machine?"

"It is," Franklin confirmed.

"So where is it?"

"Sitting in my study back in the year 1790, I presume," said Franklin. "The chamber did not follow me here. It apparently operates more like a catapult than a carriage. A bolt of lightning initiated the journey."

Tory had more questions. Franklin was more than patient. After all, meeting a time traveler was not, for most boys, an everyday occurrence.

"How are you going to get back?" asked Tory.

Franklin looked confused by the question.

Tory clarified. "I mean, in every time-travel movie I've ever seen, the people are always trying to get back."

"At the moment," said Franklin, "I have no plans of doing so. Nor do I have the means."

"Why does lightning follow you around everywhere?" asked Tory.

"For that I have no intelligent explanation," said

Franklin. "My body appears to have become a kind of lightning rod. I do not apprehend that the lightning will relent until it has sealed my doom."

"Maybe it just wants you back," said Tory.

"What do you mean?" asked Michalene.

Tory shrugged. "Since lightning brought him here, maybe it's trying to take him back to where he came from."

It took Franklin a moment to register the profundity of Tory's statement. "Well, I . . . that never occurred to me."

Franklin pondered the question a moment longer. For reasons he couldn't explain, the concept seemed perfectly logical. From the mouths of babes!

"Torrence, my boy," said Franklin. "You may be onto something."

This was all happening too fast. Tory backed up a step and shook his head vigorously. "No! I'm not onto anything. I can't even believe I'm having this conversation. That shotgun gave me brain damage!"

"Tory, he's Benjamin Franklin," Michalene reaffirmed. "Get a grip! You have to help me get him walking."

It took almost an hour, but eventually the children got Franklin to the point where he could walk on his own. Michalene couldn't help but notice that his gait was very different from that of the day before. This was the walk of a sixty-year-old man.

After Tory swallowed the fact that Benjamin Franklin was pacing his living room, he did not hesitate to express his fears about what was about to befall him. Ben Franklin or no Ben Franklin, nothing changed the fact that Tory's hours on planet earth were numbered. It was only a matter of time before that drug dealer at 1001 Shadow Place came home and discovered the empty cabinet. It likely wouldn't take the man long to suspect the involvement of Giles Peck. Besides the fact that Giles had parked his van right in front of the house, in plain sight of the neighbors, it was common knowledge that no one else in town was stupid enough to try such a thing. After the drug dealers had dealt with Giles, they would come for Tory.

Michalene agreed that Tory was in serious danger. "We have to tell the police," she said.

"No!" Tory insisted. "No cops."

Michalene scowled. "Tory, if you're worried about getting in trouble, you're acting awfully selfish right now."

"No cops!" Tory reemphasized. He softened his voice to a whisper so as not to awaken their parents. "This has nothing to do with getting in trouble. Don't you watch any of those real-life cop shows? If the police raided that house now, all they'd likely find is a lab and a few chemicals—no drugs. You may have destroyed the only evidence that would have nailed these guys. Even if they got arrested, they'd soon be out on bail looking for me. I'm not even sure the cocaine belonged to that guy on Shadow Place. For all I know, he was stashing it for somebody else—somebody from Chicago who knows exactly how to deal with punks like me."

"You're just being melodramatic," said Michalene. "They'd never hurt a thirteen-year-old kid."

Tory closed his eyes. "Sometimes, Michalene, you're so stupid I can't think up words to describe you. Do you know how much two kilos of cocaine is worth? About a hundred thousand dollars! Maybe more! For a hundred thousand dollars these people would kill their own mothers!"

"Let's be calm for the moment and think sensibly," said Franklin. "Tory, what do you propose as the best solution?"

Tory shook his head. "There is none. I'm dead. That's all there is to it."

"Don't talk like that!" cried Michalene.

"I quite agree with your sister," said Franklin. "I'm not convinced we have run out of options. It appears to me that the solution may be as simple as the nose on your face."

"Really?" said Tory.

Franklin asked them, "How does one help a man who is adrift in a rowboat in the middle of the Atlantic take his mind off the fact that he is alone and starving?"

Tory and Michalene shook their heads.

"Poke a hole in his boat," said Franklin.

"I don't get it," said Tory.

"We must convince these drug peddlers that they have a problem much more grave and immediate than the one they are facing with you. Such as the wrath of an entire community."

"Give me a break," said Tory. "You're not gonna get anybody to do anything. Nobody cares."

"I think you're wrong," said Franklin. "I think your community cares a great deal. They may simply have deluded themselves with the notion that taking care of the problem is someone else's responsibility. We must find a way to arouse them to a proper sense of obligation."

Tory's crest fell. "Great. By that time, I'll be fish food in the Mississippi River."

"That might be true," said Franklin, "if you were not so fortunate as to have a mother who works for your local periodical."

Michalene thought she'd figured out his plan. "You're gonna write an article about drug dealers in Elysia? And then you're gonna get my mother to print it?" Her tone did not sound encouraging. Even if her mother got the article in the paper, so what? It wasn't as if this would be the first article about local drug problems.

"Not just any article," Franklin clarified. "No, no, my

young friends. This will be a very special article. Children, it's time you learned the real power of the press and the wondrous benefits of a good, clean hoax."

. . .

Today is the day.

These words had resounded in Bonnie's mind at least a half dozen times as she climbed out of bed, showered, dressed, and applied her makeup. Today was the day she and Gerald would tell the children of their impending divorce.

Gerald was still asleep when she wandered into the kitchen to make herself some breakfast. The house was quiet. Mr. Benjamin and the kids must have risen with the sun. She guessed they'd gone back to the carnival. This meant Frank was doing better this morning. As well, Tory appeared to have recovered from his overdose of pizza.

As Bonnie waited for her English muffin to pop out of the toaster, the words repeated in her mind again. *Today is the day—the day we confirm what the children have likely suspected for months.* Bonnie had been dreading this day all week. Somehow, announcing it to Tory and Michalene made it all so official. After today, there was no turning back. As Bonnie spread the raspberry jam across her muffin, she was surprised to discover that her eyes were involuntarily filling with tears. This was ridiculous! She was acting like a child! *Pull yourself together!* It would all be over very soon now. If she could just get through today, she was confident that an anticipated sense of calm and relief would settle over her.

The front doorbell rang. Bonnie dabbed her eyes with a paper napkin and set the muffin on the counter. She suspected a door-to-door salesman. Perhaps Jehovah's Witnesses. After all, it was a clear, bright Saturday morning. Perfect weather for solicitors.

As she opened the door, she was surprised to find a tall, bloated man in dark sunglasses. Despite being in his thirties, the man had bad acne on his face. An emerald green Corvette was parked in the street in front of the gate. The engine was purring.

The man raised the corners of his mouth in a greasy smile. "Is Tory here?"

"I'm afraid not," Bonnie replied. "The kids were gone when I got up this morning. I wish I had their energy."

"Yes." The man craned his neck around Bonnie and looked into the house, as if he didn't trust her. "Do you know where he might have gone, or when he might be back?"

Bonnie shook her head. "Is there something I can help you with?"

"No, no," said the man. He reached into his breast pocket. "But I wonder if you could take my card." Bonnie took it. The card had no name; just a phone number. "I can be reached at that number day or night. Have him call me as soon as he gets home. It's very important."

"Is Tory in some sort of trouble?" asked Bonnie.

The man chuckled. He tried to appear casual. He tried too hard. "Of course not. You just have him call me."

The man stepped off the porch and retreated toward his car.

"Can I tell him your name?" Bonnie shouted.

The man didn't even glance back. He slipped through the gate and climbed into the passenger's side of the Corvette, pretending he hadn't heard Bonnie call out to him. He almost acted as if knocking on the door had been a mistake. The Corvette sped off down the street.

Bonnie looked again at the number on the card. What could a fat man in a green Corvette possibly want from her son? She wondered if Tory had sold his father's bicycle. The boy had tried to sell it to strangers before. Maybe the man was an undercover police officer seeking to ask Tory some questions about things that *other* boys had done. Maybe this was all part of a surprise she wasn't supposed to know about. Bonnie was desperate to believe any answer that would not add more stress to her life. She was not about to consider that her son's life was in serious danger.

• • •

Franklin and the children spent the day inside the small public library on Adams Street. It may not have had a large selection of Franklin biographies, but its selection of current periodicals was adequate for Franklin's needs. While Michalene looked up references, Tory fetched the various issues. Franklin wanted to learn as much as he could about America's illegal drug trade. He read about twenty different articles in *Time, Newsweek,* and *U.S. News & World Report.* Certainly he did not expect these articles to make him any kind of expert, but they gave him just enough information to meet the task at hand.

Franklin also studied a dozen or so back issues of the local biweekly *Gazette.* In it he found two recent articles on Elysia's drug epidemic, but even more interesting was a recent pattern he discovered with respect to the opinion page. This page included a regular column dedicated to community appreciation. Local businesses used this space to express their thanks to the people of Elysia. Ofttimes these businesses would single out certain groups, individuals, and employees and thank them publicly for support or contributions that had helped them to boost profits or morale. The letters also gave the businesses a chance to mention any contributions they happened to have made to the community, such as donations to clubs, organizations, and city projects.

It was all a public relations thing, and Franklin was amused to see how the various businesses tried to outdo one another. He decided that his particular letter would outdo them all.

Michalene was kind enough to help Franklin with the wording in a few places to ensure the use of modern vernacular; otherwise, the letter was pure Franklin. Michalene and Tory went home about five o'clock, but Franklin decided to remain at the library to put his final touches on what might prove to be the final hoax of his life.

Franklin would have been hard-pressed to count all of the hoaxes he had perpetrated over the years. Hoaxes had been one of his most successful devices for swaying public opinion. It had been only about a month since he'd penned what he previously thought would be his last hoax. This recent hoax, published in the *Federal Gazette,* had been designed to sting the consciences of certain individuals in Congress who were attempting to prove that slavery was an institution sanctioned by the Holy Bible and that Negroes were better off and happier as slaves. Franklin's response was to publish an essay by one "Sidi Mehemet Ibrahim," a leading member of the government of Algeria, who used the same sort of logic on the Algerian people to justify the enslavement of white Christians. Sidi Mehemet Ibrahim may have been the fictional creation of Benjamin Franklin, but the letter still produced its desired effect, which was to show how pathetically inane such logic really was. Franklin's objectives today were equally direct—to sting the conscience of the entire community of Elysia, Illinois.

The letter read as follows:

To all my customers, friends, and supporters—in short, to the entire community of Elysia, Illinois. From Mr. I. M. Happiness, your local distributor of recreational substances:

Since the time has come that my particular vocation is receiving more acceptance than ever before, I would feel wholly ungrateful if I did not add my voice to the voices of every other successful merchant and businessman in Elysia for helping me to achieve yet another record-breaking year in sales. In 1993, a whopping 35% of all my 1992 customers have advanced from their use of milder substances to a regular consumption of my finest, top-of-the line products, proving once and for all that my first and foremost concern is customer satisfaction. Cocaine sales, especially, have jumped so dramatically in 1993 that my suppliers in Chicago can hardly keep up with the demand. Thanks to your support, I am now able to offer my products to a wider range of customers than ever before. As my way of saying "thank you," I am now providing, for an unlimited time, one free sample of each of my products to any new patron. I present this offer regardless of age, sex, race, or circumstances.

As you know, I have always been one of Elysia's most outspoken equal-opportunity employers, restoring dignity and self-respect to the poor and downtrodden of our fair community. I am always particularly mindful of our wayward youth. Each year I have been fortunate enough to recruit a younger and more talented sales force. This year we expect a booming return from our efforts in the community's local grade schools—an environment that has proven surprisingly receptive and enthusiastic.

My heartiest appreciation must go out to you parents of these eager youngsters. Many of you are faithful customers yourselves, or else have granted to your children at an early age that independence so necessary these days to make it as adults, thus allowing you to diligently pursue all your other interests, career and so forth, or to simply enjoy all those deserved hours of relaxation in front of the television.

It's an unfortunate fact that misery and failure are rampant in our world. No one enjoys being on the receiving end of abuse or neglect, least of all me. But I've come to accept that such things are an unavoidable part of life. We cannot deny that more and more parents—mothers and fathers alike—are forced by overwhelming pressure to abandon spouse and family in order to meet their basic and primal needs for freedom and variety. No problem! Isn't it comforting to know that all of our most fundamental human requirements—love, pleasure, happiness, and security—can be so easily replaced by the frequent use of our products?

I will always be deeply indebted to our prison system. My best employees continue to be graduates of the complimentary training programs provided in these institutions. I am, after all, a proud graduate myself, having learned many important aspects of my trade while thus incarcerated. For those seeking a serious career in my field, I cannot recommend these programs enough.

I would feel most unkind if I forgot to express my appreciation to those police and community leaders who continually place greater emphasis on harsher punishments and severer penalties than on those futile programs of treatment, prevention, and education. At first it might seem ironic that I would feel grateful for this, but I have found that such an approach by police and politicians generally encourages the feelings of despair and bitterness toward society that lead people to seek out our services in the first place. As well, I've noticed that all the tax money spent in apprehending and prosecuting people in our industry tends to weed out incompetence. It also provides us with a wonderful incentive to improve

197

our methods of conducting business and to invest in the latest and most sophisticated technologies. My motto is: As long as you folks want what we have to offer, come hell or high water we'll find a way to get it to you.

So as I relax here in my lovely home, situated comfortably for a millennium plus one in this shadowy place, I want the citizens of Elysia to know how much I realize that without you, none of my success would have been possible. Thank you for making me such an integral part of your local economy. I apologize for having to use a false name. Each day I feel we grow closer to the time when pseudonyms will no longer be necessary.

I promise you that as long as I live in your community, I will do my utmost to serve and to be of service. You can depend on me, O Elysians. Because of all the faithful customers I have established over the years, you are virtually guaranteed that even if I am forced to retire for some unforeseen reason, another merchant will swiftly arrive to take my place. My door is always open to you. And remember—your children are my children.

Sincerely,

I. M. Happiness

Franklin could only hope that his subtle insertion of the drug dealer's address in the second-to-last paragraph would be recognized by someone of importance. He knew, however, that if he were to include the address boldly and clearly, the letter would not get printed. Maybe he could have Michalene or Tory discreetly point out the clue after the letter hit the paper.

Now it was just a matter of getting the letter onto Bonnie

Mickelson's desk at the *Elysia Gazette.* If he sent it through the mail it might arrive by Monday. With any luck, it would be printed in the very next edition on Tuesday afternoon.

Good heavens! thought Franklin. Tuesday was three days away! Tory's prediction that by then he might be "fish food" in the Mississippi River might not have been as facetious as it sounded. Franklin figured he had two, maybe three, days before old age did him in. If he could protect Tory until Tuesday it might be enough.

As Franklin stood up to start back to the Mickelsons' house, he was reminded how difficult this was going to be. Even the act of standing demonstrated his feeble age. By morning he would be well over seventy years old! He couldn't worry about this now. He had to get home. He had to return to the presence of Tory Mickelson as quickly as possible.

CHAPTER 15

This was big.

Tory decided it was much too big for their local television station. In fact, it was big enough for one of the major
networks. Dan Rather and Connie Chung! But since Tory
had no idea how to call those guys, he went to the private
phone in his father's den and dialed Channel 9 in Chicago.
After being transferred about the station for a while, he
finally got someone who claimed to be in the news department. Michalene wandered by the den in time to hear the tail
end of the conversation.

"No, no! Benjamin Franklin!" Tory yelled into the
phone. "Yes! Haven't you ever heard of Benjamin Franklin?
. . . In my home *right now!* . . . Like I said, he came when
lightning struck his time machine . . . I'm totally serious! . . .
I *know* how it sounds. Don't you think— . . . Listen I— . . .
Just let me— . . . " Tory pulled the phone away from his ear
and yelled into the mouthpiece. "You're losin' out on a lotta
money, pal!" He slammed down the receiver. "Jerk!"

When Tory noticed Michalene in the doorway, his face
reddened. "Oh, hi."

"What did you think you were doing?" she demanded.

"Nothin', I—" He sighed. "Oh, they weren't interested
anyway. They thought I was a lunatic!"

Michalene pointed a stern finger at her brother. "Don't

200

ever try that again. When Mr. Franklin wants to make the world aware of who he is, he'll let us know. He'll probably do it himself."

"What difference does it make if it's now or later?" asked Tory. "We could make *millions* off this!"

"Millions off what?" Bonnie Mickelson now stood behind Michalene.

"Nothing, Mom," said Michalene. "Tory was just shooting his mouth off."

Bonnie recalled the man at the door. "Which reminds me," she said to Tory. "There was a man looking for you today."

Tory's face whitened. "Looking for me?"

"Yes. A man in a green Corvette. He wouldn't tell me what he wanted."

Tory shook his head. "I don't know either, Mom. One of my friends' dads, I suppose, looking for his kid."

Bonnie might have pursued it further if the subject on her mind had not been so heavy. "Anyway . . . " She took a deep breath. "Your father and I have something we'd like to discuss with both of you. Could you come into the living room?"

The children looked at one another, shrugged, and followed her out. Tory guessed they were about to discuss the best way to kick Frank Benjamin out of the house. Michalene was a little more perceptive. *Here it comes,* she thought. *This is finally it.* She consoled herself by thinking it was about time.

Bonnie was surprised to see Gerald standing near the front door with the car keys dangling from his hand.

"Let's all go for a ride," Gerald suggested. "We can talk over Chinese food. Sound good?"

Bonnie looked disappointed. She had hoped to get this

over with quickly. But she decided there might be wisdom in her husband's approach. Maybe the social atmosphere would soften the blow. Yet it also seemed deceptive—creating the illusion of a fun family outing and then dropping such a bombshell.

As everyone started toward the car, the phone rang. Gerald answered. It was for Tory.

"Hurry up," he told his son, handing him the receiver. "We'll be in the car."

Tory watched his family exit the house before putting the phone to his ear. "Hello?"

The voice on the other end wasted no time with introductions. "Listen to me, you little————! If I don't get those bricks back by tonight, you're dead! You understand me? I'll rip your throat out! Do you hear what I'm telling—?"

Tory hung up the phone. He stared straight ahead for several seconds, shaking and sucking deep breaths. He closed his eyes and tried to pull himself together. *When we get home from the restaurant,* he thought, *I'll go away . . . I'll go away and never come back.*

• • •

It was almost dark as Franklin rolled his bicycle into the Mickelsons' driveway. The hoax letter was folded up in his back pocket. During the ride home he decided it was time to confront Bonnie and Gerald. It was time to tell them who he was. He didn't think it would take much to convince them of the truth. How many people might they know who had aged twenty-eight years in two days? Franklin had also decided to hand the letter over to Bonnie directly. He couldn't risk any unforeseen delays that might forestall the letter's publication. Surely after Bonnie had read the letter and listened to Franklin's explanation for having written it, she would do all she could to see that it came out in Tuesday's edition.

Franklin climbed off the bike and parked it along the side of the house. He had to confess, his muscles and joints just didn't seem to move the way they had the past couple of days. The last time he had been sixty years old was around the time he stood before the House of Commons in his fight to see the Stamp Act repealed. He distinctly remembered his body being in much better shape in 1766 than it was today. Perhaps he was a little older than he'd first estimated. Or perhaps this merciless age acceleration was exacting an unnatural toll on his constitution.

The house was still. Franklin noticed that the car was gone from the driveway. The family was off somewhere. He recalled what Bonnie had told him about their plans to announce the divorce to the children tonight.

Franklin felt awkward about entering the house alone, almost as if he were trespassing. He decided that if he wasn't a legitimate house guest by now, he never would be. He turned the door knob. *Hmmm.* The front door was locked.

No matter. He made his way around to the back. If this entrance was also locked, he would simply wait on the front lawn and enjoy the appearance of the stars. It might be enlightening to see if the constellations were still in the same patterns as two hundred years ago.

Franklin rounded the corner of the house. He expected the Mickelsons' dog, Joker, to begin a fanfare of barking. Curiously, the dog on its chain was perfectly content. It crouched near its doghouse, every ounce of attention focused on a pair of raw T-bone steaks. A rather generous dinner offering, Franklin thought. But at least he did not have to endure that infernal barking.

He approached the back door. The screen had been torn.

Had it been like that before? Then he noticed that the lock had been broken. The door fell open under a push of his hand. He stepped inside and examined the lock more closely.

By the time Franklin realized what was happening, it was too late. Even before he heard footsteps approaching from behind, it occurred to him why the dog was eating T-bones. Apparently someone else had been concerned with the animal's loud barking.

Franklin moved to turn, but before he could, something hard and heavy struck him on the back of the head.

• • •

Tory and Michalene didn't have much to say during the ride home. What *could* they say? Would saying anything have made any difference? Every detail of the plan had already been laid out. No one had asked them for input. It was clear that any ideas they might have suggested would have been rejected anyway.

Dad was moving out on the first day of September. Mom's job at the newspaper expanded to full time as soon as the kids started school. Dad would see them every other weekend, one month during the summer, and every other holiday. They made it all sound so clear-cut and uncomplicated, almost . . . natural.

The news shocked Tory more than he expected. He nearly forgot that someone had threatened his life earlier that same day. The boy decided it was all a sign. Running away from home made no difference now. Dying didn't seem to make any difference either. What hurt him most was that his father didn't even ask him if he wanted to come live with him. Even if Tory had refused on account of his mother's sad eyes, just the offer would have made all the difference in the world.

Michalene started crying as they exited the restaurant. All the emotional preparation in the world hadn't softened the blow. Bonnie sat with her in the back seat. Tory sat up front with his father. During the drive home, Gerald tried to change the subject and talk about the lightning incidents that had occurred earlier in the week. He told them how the new paint job on the Bonneville would cost eleven hundred dollars. Thank goodness insurance would cover most of it. When Gerald realized that no one was really paying attention, he reached over and put his hand on Tory's knee.

"You doin' all right, sport?"

Tory stared out the window. "Sure, Dad. I'm doin' fine."

"Don't look so down," said Gerald.

"I'm not down," said Tory. "Like you said, it's all for the better."

As Gerald turned onto their street, they heard sirens approaching, wailing. Gerald pulled over to the side of the road and allowed two fire engines and an ambulance to pass them by. Whenever Gerald heard sirens in his life, he couldn't help but wonder if this was finally the one racing toward his own house. As an adult, he'd never taken such thoughts seriously, but their occurrence was unavoidable. When Gerald noticed that the fire trucks had stopped in front of his property, he still refused to believe it. The odds were too staggering. Only after reaching his own driveway, where he could see the smoke and the flames and the firemen crashing through the front door, did he face reality.

Pandemonium gripped the Mickelsons' car. Gerald leaped out yelling, "How did it happen? How did it happen?"

The house was not yet engulfed. A neighbor had noticed flames consuming the living room curtains and called 911. The fire department appeared to have arrived in time. Joker barked wildly. Gerald slipped around to the back of the house before anyone could stop him. One of the men pulled Bonnie aside.

"Is anyone inside the house?" he demanded.

"Frank might be in there!" cried Michalene.

The fireman passed on the information. Bonnie and the children watched two more firemen storm through the front door while others dragged fire hoses across the lawn. After a few moments, the two firemen emerged. They were helping a man. The man's arms were full of equipment—a computer terminal and monitor. Bonnie and the children were dumbfounded when they realized the rescued victim was Gerald! He'd gone inside the back door!

When Gerald was far enough from the house, he knelt down, coughing, and set his computer equipment on the lawn. Paramedics surrounded him. He brushed them off, insisting that he was perfectly all right. After a moment, the paramedics were convinced and left him alone. Gerald continued to kneel on the grass and catch his breath. When he finally looked up, the face of his wife glowered down at him.

"You rushed into a burning house," said Bonnie, "and risked your life . . . for a *computer?*"

"I've got everything on this computer," Gerald defended limply. "All my documents. Everything for the meeting on Monday in Dallas. I leave for O'Hare tomorrow at noon, you know. The house is insured. These documents are not."

Bonnie put one hand over her mouth and closed her eyes. She shook her head slowly and let the hand drop. "Up until this moment," she began, "up until this *very instant,* I never realized what a selfish and shallow human being you really are. My marriage may be ending, my home may be burning, but for the first time in months, I feel peace. Thank you, Gerald, for making this so clear to me tonight."

Gerald's eyebrows lifted. He'd never heard his wife speak so bluntly. Bonnie walked back toward the children. Still panting and coughing, Gerald looked down at his computer. Suddenly, for the life of him, he could not recall the impulse that had led him to do such a stupid thing.

A fireman approached. "We can't find anyone else in the house."

"Maybe Frank is still at the library," said Michalene.

"We've almost got it under control," the fireman continued. "Only the front room appears to have sustained major damage. You folks are lucky. We're certain this is the work of a burglar or an arsonist."

"Arson?" Bonnie couldn't believe it! "Who would want to burn down our house?"

"I wouldn't know, ma'am," said the fireman. "But the place was trashed before the fire was set. It looked as if somebody was looking for something. Do you have any idea what they might have been looking for?"

"No idea," Bonnie replied. "No idea whatsoever."

The fireman considered her again, nodded, and went back to work.

Michalene knew what the arsonists had been looking for. Her eyes searched for Tory. Where was he? He'd been standing right next to her only a second ago.

Michalene called out. "Tory!"

Bonnie and Gerald started looking around as well. They joined Michalene in shouting Tory's name. No one responded. Tory had managed to slip off into the darkness.

• • •

From the cornfield just west of the Mickelsons' home, Benjamin Franklin watched Tory scurry down the street. Franklin reached up and massaged the bump on the back of his head. Just as his other bump was healing, it had been topped with a new one.

But the blow did not knock him unconscious. He only pretended to be unconscious while drawers were pulled open and furniture was turned upside down. The instant Franklin felt certain his assailants were in other rooms, he staggered to his feet and fled out the back door. It was when he entered the cornfield that he started to feel dizzy. He wasn't exactly sure when he fainted. One moment he was running, the next he was face down in the dirt.

He must have lain there for several minutes before regaining coherency. Even such a short period of unconsciousness had brought an excruciating stiffness to his muscles and joints. The stiffness, however, was not wholly paralyzing. He could move his arms and legs just enough to work it out by himself. In ten or fifteen minutes, he felt certain he'd be able to stand and walk. Franklin would not have been surprised to discover that he was two or three years older in appearance.

Shortly, he heard the sirens of the fire trucks and he smelled the smoke. When at last he made it to his feet, his first impulse was to return to the house. Seeing Tory dash down the street changed his mind. There was no time to lose. Franklin started after him. Tory had fled in the direction of the river.

It was several minutes before Franklin's leg muscles worked at normal capacity. He continued his pursuit at a modest jog. Franklin knew where Tory was going. He hoped he wasn't too late. Thank goodness it was night. He remembered distinctly that the sun had been bright and shining as Tory fell from that pipe. As long as it was dark, his chances of averting this disaster still seemed possible.

Franklin continued on for over a mile before reaching

the path through the weeds that led down to Tory's beloved spot overlooking the waters of the spillway. His heart was pounding relentlessly as he crashed through the brush, finally reaching the small clearing beyond the trees where the pipe came out of the earth and stretched across the river.

But Tory was not here! Had Franklin been moving so quickly that he'd overtaken the lad? He'd felt certain that the boy was headed in this direction. Every instinct flowing in his veins had confirmed it. Franklin searched the area. He walked back to the road. Tory was nowhere in sight.

His panting had turned into wheezing. His energy was spent. Even if the boy was not here now, he was bound to arrive any moment. The philosopher sat himself down where the path opened into the clearing. He would wait here until Tory arrived—all night if necessary. Hopefully no lightning storms were due before morning. Even if what Tory had suggested was true—that the lightning was trying to reclaim him—to be reclaimed before he could right the wrong he may have caused America's future would be the most terrible tragedy of his life. Gradually, Franklin's breathing got easier. His heart rate slowed. Oh, but he felt so tired. So exhausted. If only he could . . . sleep . . .

No! Franklin shook himself. He *couldn't* fall asleep. Not now! Why was he so tired all of a sudden? Why couldn't he control it? Throughout Franklin's life, whenever a critical situation had demanded that he shed every whit of lassitude and remain awake and alert, he had never failed to do so. What was happening to him?

To grow older by fourteen years every night, to suffer excruciating stiffness every morning—he could endure all of this without complaint. After all, these last few days had been the gracious gift of an all-loving Creator. But to lose his self-will, to relinquish the mastery of his own flesh and spirit—this was almost too much to bear. Oddly, Franklin found himself reflecting on an old story from the New Testament, one he'd pondered as child. It had always bothered him that the night before the crucifixion the apostles had slept in spite of Christ's admonition that he needed them to be with him.

Never! Franklin cried in his heart. *I would have never slept. Not if my very life depended on it. Never . . . I would . . . I would . . . have . . . never . . .*

Franklin's eyelids dropped.

CHAPTER 16

There was a rumbling on the hill above. It took exceeding effort for Franklin to lift the lids of his eyes—like opening a sealed crypt. It was daytime. By the position of the blurry sun, he guessed it was just before nine. His eyes fought to stay focused. He couldn't tell who or what was scuffling down the hill, sending small rocks tripping to the bottom.

Franklin was totally paralyzed. The only muscles that had not atrophied overnight controlled his lungs. Breathing was easy enough, likely because his ever-working lungs had never stopped to stiffen. He'd fallen asleep with his neck bent and his eyes aimed in the direction of the cliff. The pipe that stretched across the river was directly in his view. If only his eyes would focus, he could easily tell who or what had created the noise. His focus improved enough to sense a shape sliding down from the railroad tracks. The figure's upper body had a red tinge. He knew it must be Tory. The lad was wearing the same red shirt he had on the day before.

Franklin tried to speak. Only a hollow gasp emerged. His tongue was also stiff and numb. The boy hadn't noticed him lying at the place where the path opened into the clearing. Franklin's body was only partially hidden by undergrowth. If Tory turned around, Franklin could easily be seen.

His focus improved further. The figure was definitely Tory. Why hadn't the boy arrived by way of the path? He'd reached the clearing by wandering along the railroad tracks and sliding down the hill. He suspected the boy had spent the night huddled in the quiet corner of someone's hay field—if in fact he had slept at all.

After Tory reached the bottom, he wandered over to the pipe. He lay back across it and stared upward at the sky. Franklin tried to call out again. The gasp in his throat was no louder than before.

After a few minutes, Tory turned over on his stomach and gazed into the waters of the spillway. In another moment, he pushed himself up and began his balancing act to the edge of the cliff. Franklin felt a surge of panic. Again he tried to call out. If not for the spillway's roar, Franklin felt certain this time he would have been heard. Why wouldn't the boy just look in his direction?

It was hopeless. Despite all Franklin's efforts, he would be forced to watch helplessly as destiny played out its course. He could do no more for the boy now than he could before—when the springboard of time had tossed him back and forth.

Tory grabbed both steel cables in both hands and stared long and hard at the churning waters. He drew a deep breath. Franklin watched him sit down beyond the first set of cables and straddle the pipe with his legs. He lay on his stomach.

Franklin made his first audible sound—"Tor—! Tor—!"—but his voice was still no more than a hoarse whisper.

Tory locked his legs together beneath the pipe and began to scoot forward, inch by inch. He was well out over the river now. There was no going back. To turn around would have been more dangerous than sliding forward.

What could possibly be going through the boy's mind? Franklin wondered. *Was Tory trying to kill himself?* As a typical thrill-seeking youngster, Tory Mickelson had likely felt tempted by that pipe all of his life. His friends had probably teased each other whenever they came together about venturing out there. During those moments when Tory had sat in this place alone, listening to the waters of the spillway, he'd probably dared himself more times than he could count. What effect had the events of the previous two days had upon Tory's sense of reason? Was he accepting his own dare? Did the pipe represent a twisted kind of victory for the lad? Proof that there were no unconquerable things in this world? Why, *why,* would anyone attempt such an irrational thing?

Tory made it to the next set of cables, a full ten feet out over the river. He stopped there for a moment, assessing his success. Encouraged, the boy began the journey to the next set of cables, twenty feet out over the churning waters.

"Torrreee! Torrreeé!" Had Tory been back at the place where the pipe came out of the hill, he would have clearly heard Franklin's graveled voice. Now, so far out over the spillway, it was impossible. In agony, Franklin watched him arrive at the third set of cables. And then the fourth.

Tory was now forty feet out over the river. The pipe had become slick. In spite of that slickness, the boy set out for the next set of cables. His progress was much slower. There were long pauses when he didn't move at all, clinging tenaciously to the pipe for dear life, working up his nerve to continue. *Why am I doing this?* he thought. Yet he'd already made it a full third of the entire journey. *One third!* Tory had never heard of anyone making it out so far before!

"Tory! Tory!" Franklin's voice had almost reached normal volume, but it still wasn't enough to override the spillway's roar. What did it matter now if Tory heard him or not? The boy was fifty feet out over the water. At any moment, Tory Mickelson would fall. The life of what might have been

213

a future president of the United States was about to end in a most foolish and tragic manner. And, like six days ago, Benjamin Franklin would watch in utter helplessness.

The first sign of trouble began as Tory set out to reach the next set of cables. The pipe was extremely slick now. Tory hadn't considered how cold it would be. The rising mist had soaked his clothes. The pipe itself was very cold. His skin was starting to numb. There were several instances, as he sought to reach that sixth set of cables, when he nearly slipped. Toward the end of this ten-foot stretch, he was much too hasty. He reached out to grab the cables from too great a distance. His legs started to slide. He caught the cable, but his body rolled underneath the pipe. With his ankles locked together, he clung with one arm and both legs. Franklin gasped. The lock on Tory's ankles held only a few seconds—just enough time for the boy to grip the cable in the crook of his arm.

His legs dropped. Tory reached up his other hand. He hung there for an eternity, his arm pinched at the elbow between the pipe and the cable. A surge of energy helped him hoist himself up, but it was clear by the way he held his arm that it had been injured, somehow twisted as he caught himself. The boy had gone as far as he could go, forward or backward.

Franklin's voice was fully restored. He tried calling Tory's name one final time. The waters of the spillway were just too loud. From the place on the ground where Franklin lay paralyzed, it looked to him as if Tory stared long and hard down at the river, wondering if he should just give up and drop.

"Mr. Franklin!"

Franklin rolled his eyes to see who had spoken. "Michalene? Is that you, my dear?"

He also saw Gerald standing over him. They had been searching for Tory and Franklin most of the night.

"Holy—! What—what happened to you, Frank?" asked Gerald.

"I told you, Dad," said Michalene. "I told you."

Bonnie was there too. She took in Franklin's features from head to toe. "I don't understand. He must be almost eighty years old!"

"Now do you believe me?" asked Michalene. "He *is* Benjamin Franklin."

"Never mind me," said Franklin. "Your son—Tory—he's out over the river."

When Bonnie caught sight of her son sixty feet out over the spillway, she nearly lost her senses. All the bitter, black memories of her little girl drowning in this river came rushing back. Gerald started frantically screaming Tory's name. The boy heard, then turned his face away in shame.

Gerald ran to the edge of the cliff. He screamed at his son. "Of all the—! In heaven's name, what are you doing?"

Tory still refused to speak.

Gerald turned back to Bonnie. "Call 911! Hurry!"

Bonnie dashed back to the car. Michalene remained with Franklin.

Again, Gerald called out to Tory. "Can you crawl back by yourself?"

The boy shook his head.

"Okay, okay! Don't move! Just hang on, son! Help is on the way!" Gerald stepped back toward Franklin and Michalene. He glared down at the grizzled philosopher. "Why has Tory done this?" Without waiting for a reply, he gestured toward Franklin and said to Michalene, "What's the matter with him? Why can't he move?"

"I tried to explain to you," said Michalene. "Every morning his joints stiffen up. They need to be worked loose."

"I fell asleep here," Franklin explained, "while awaiting Tory's arrival. I knew he would come here."

"Why didn't you stop him?" Gerald demanded. "Why would he do this? What asinine ideas did you put into his head?"

"It's not his fault, Dad!" Michalene defended. "Did you already forget who this man is?"

"None of this makes sense!" Gerald pressed his fists to his temples. "Why is this happening today? I have a plane to catch in five hours!"

Michalene scowled at her father. "That's all you care about, isn't it? You don't even care that Tory might fall!"

"He's *not* gonna fall!" Gerald stepped back over to the edge of the cliff. "Tory, are you doing all right?"

Tory spoke his first words. "My arm!" he called back. "I hurt it!"

The injured arm was the same one that feebly gripped the cable. Since the other arm was situated on the far side, away from the cables, it could offer only limited support.

"Can you hold on?" asked Gerald.

"I don't know!" said Tory.

"Can you bring your leg up over the cable and hold on with the other arm?"

Tory had already asked himself the same question moments earlier. His answer was no. Fear had frozen the boy. He didn't dare move a muscle.

"I can't!" Tory called back.

Gerald tried to think. He knew that his wife was still three minutes away from a phone.

"Just hang on, Tory!" Gerald pleaded. "Help will be here in a few minutes!"

Gerald began pacing nervously. The danger was more immediate than he'd first suspected. If Tory's arm had not been injured, the boy might have perched himself there for hours. As Gerald squinted, he thought perhaps he could see blood on the boy's sleeve.

Michalene busily worked to loosen Franklin's joints.

"It *is* my fault," Franklin proclaimed.

"How is it your fault?" said Michalene. "You couldn't have stopped him in the condition you're in."

"No," said Franklin. "That day we were here. All my talk about values. My silly analogy of the pipe."

Michalene shook her head. "I don't follow you."

"I think I understand now," said Franklin, "perhaps even better than Tory understands himself. Don't you see, my dear? Tory is the value. Who will climb out onto that pipe for *him?*"

Gerald stepped over to Franklin and Michalene again. He was pale.

"He—he says his arm is injured. He doesn't know if he can hold on. How can I—? I don't know what to do. What can I do?"

Franklin and Michalene looked up at Gerald. The man was shaking like a leaf. Neither Franklin nor Michalene had an answer for him.

Tory cried out again. "DAD!"

Gerald leaped back toward the edge of the cliff. "What is it, Tory?"

"It hurts!" Tory continued to weep. "It hurts so bad!"

Gerald could see it now. Blood had streamed down Tory's arm. It was dripping from the pipe, disappearing into the churning mist.

Gerald started to panic. "Please, God, no! Don't let go, Tory! Please, don't let go!"

"I'm scared, Dad!" Tory cried. "I'm scared! I'm scared . . . "

At that moment, Gerald saw Tory as a teary-eyed five-year-old again, frightened of the dark. So innocent. So dependent. So fragile. No more hesitation. He'd lost one child in this river. He wasn't about to lose another.

Gerald grabbed the first set of cables. The prospects of survival for a boy on this pipe were much more promising than the same prospects for an adult. For someone of Gerald's weight and physical shape, such an act could be judged as nothing less than suicide. After all, the pipe was only ten inches in diameter. Gerald swung his leg over the pipe and lay down on his stomach. The length of pipe between the first and second cables sagged and creaked. At several of the joints, it began leaking water.

"Hang on, Tory!" Gerald cried. "I'm coming!"

Gerald made it to the second set of cables without a problem. However, it took him twice the time it had taken Tory. Gerald's weight caused the pipe to swing, making Tory less stable than before.

"I'm falling!" Tory cried.

"No!" Gerald screamed. "Just one more minute! You have to hang on for *one more minute!*"

During his journey to the third set of cables, Gerald slipped, rolling underneath the pipe. His legs and arms remained locked around the top. Michalene screamed. Her father scooted forward as he hugged the metal from underneath. He reached the next pair of cables. It took every ounce of Gerald's strength to pull himself back over the top. Michalene was certain now she would lose not only a brother this day, but a father as well.

Franklin was confused. Before, when he had first seen Tory fall from that pipe, Gerald had not been in the picture at all. This was all wrong. *Anything* could happen.

Gerald reached the fourth set of cables without a close

call. He thought he had a system now. The trick was to cross his feet on top of the pipe and scoot along two or three inches at a time. But the pipe was getting slicker.

"Are you doing okay?" Gerald called over to his son.

"I can't hold it!" the boy cried.

"You *have* to hold it!"

Gerald had only twenty feet remaining. Each time before scooting forward, he reached ahead and tried to scrape off the slick film that clung to the pipe. The rising mist had soaked him to the bone. The pipe was creaking worse. Nearly every joint started leaking as Gerald proceeded. Bonnie arrived back at the clearing. She gasped at the sight of her husband and son. There were sirens in the distance.

"What is Gerald doing?" Bonnie demanded.

"Tory is slipping, Mom," said Michalene gravely.

Franklin's muscles had been loosened enough for him to sit up. The three of them watched breathlessly as Gerald made his way to the fifth set of cables. Only ten feet were left. If Gerald could just make it this last ten feet . . .

"I can't feel my arm, Dad," Tory whimpered.

Gerald could clearly see the blood dripping from the pipe. A broken strand in the cable's twine had deeply sliced Tory's tricep.

"Just lock it around that cable," said Gerald. "I'm almost there. I'm almost there."

As Gerald set out on the last leg of his journey, Tory repeated over and over, "I'm sorry, Dad. I'm sorry."

"Don't worry, Son," Gerald responded. "I'm almost there."

From three feet away, Gerald reached out his hand. He grabbed Tory's belt. He knew this would not help the boy. It only meant that if Tory fell, Gerald would fall with him. It was the touch that was so important to Gerald. It meant that he had made it. It also strengthened Tory. His father had come. Tory found the courage to hang on another few seconds. Gerald gained the strength to pull himself forward, grip one cable and then the other, and then embrace his son between them.

Franklin, Bonnie, and Michalene shrieked ecstatically through joyful tears. Gerald held Tory in his arms. His son continued apologizing.

"It's okay," Gerald assured him. "It's okay now."

Tory couldn't look into his father's eyes. "I saw her fall, Dad. I never told anyone. I saw her fall."

"What?"

"Carolyn," said Tory. "I was here. I told her not to play on the pipe. I told her to go home. She wanted to be like me. I turned around for just a second. She just wanted to be like me. I'm *sooo* sorry."

Tory's sobbing intensified. Gerald cried too. He couldn't imagine what it must have been like for the boy to carry around such a burden for so long. Gerald did not judge himself blameless. He had long suspected that Tory knew what had happened that day, and he punished the boy in small, subtle ways for not telling. By the tone in his voice. By those brief, poisonous looks. Because Gerald hurt too, he'd successfully intensified the guilt in his son. Had a parent ever done a more reprehensible thing to a child? At the moment, Gerald didn't think so.

Despite the pain pulsing in his heart, Gerald couldn't deny that something had been reborn inside him. Something had come alive the moment he climbed onto that pipe—a thing he'd thought was long since dead and beyond resuscitation.

With his elbow hooked around the cable, Gerald stroked his son's wet hair. "It's all right now," Gerald said. "Everything is going to be all right."

CHAPTER 17

The rescue concluded a little after 11:00 A.M. Rescuers stood atop the railroad bridge and dropped down a harness. Gerald strapped his son into the harness first. The cut on Tory's arm was severe. He'd lost at least two pints of blood. Gerald was hoisted up just as an ambulance rushed his son off to the hospital.

Michalene worked with Franklin to get him walking. The philosopher had almost fully recovered by the time the paramedics inquired if they could be of assistance.

"That's very kind of you to offer," said Franklin, "but I believe this young lady has worked a miracle."

The paramedics were the same two men who had helped Franklin the night he was hit by the Mickelsons' car. One of them looked Franklin over with a strange sense of recognition.

"You look like somebody," the paramedic said.

"Indeed? Who?" asked Franklin.

The paramedic thought a moment longer. "George Washington," he replied. "Has anyone ever told you that you look exactly like George Washington?"

"Not recently," said Franklin.

Neither of the men considered that he might be the same person they'd treated a few days before.

Michalene's efforts to restore Franklin's strength had

understandably limited results. At seventy-eight years of age (give or take a year) his muscles and joints were enervated. Franklin felt certain that the deterioration he'd experienced over the last several days was significantly more crippling than the natural deterioration of aging. Or if not worse, different somehow. Franklin thought it felt more like overexertion than old age. Whatever the case, Franklin—as well as Michalene—seemed to know instinctively that this was his last day. Tonight, if he lived that long, he would surely pass away in his sleep.

Franklin spent the next hour with Michalene, Gerald, and Bonnie in the waiting area of the hospital's emergency room. The nurse told them that Tory was doing fine. The doctor would be finished shortly. Tory would be free to go home.

Gerald and Bonnie looked utterly exhausted. They still wore yesterday's clothes. Bonnie fell asleep. The only pillow she could find was her husband's shoulder. Michalene thought at first that her father might move over one place and allow her to sleep on the seat. For a second, Gerald actually considered it. Bonnie's gesture had taken him by surprise. He didn't know quite how to react. He sighed and brought his arm around his wife's waist.

Franklin and Michalene were seated across the aisle. Gerald caught the look on his daughter's face. He could read her thoughts—*So what does this mean, Dad?* He sent back a quirked expression, smiling on one side of his mouth, as if to say, *I'm really not sure what this means.*

Then he met the eyes of Benjamin Franklin. Franklin wore a wide grin. Gerald became uncomfortable and looked away. It still hadn't fully registered in his mind who this man was.

Finally, Gerald looked back and said, "My daughter told

me everything that happened the other night. I want to thank you for what you did for my children, especially what you did for Tory."

"Not at all," said Franklin. "Your children are among the brightest and most promising I have ever known."

Gerald looked Franklin over again. After biting his lip, he said, "I know who my son and daughter think you are . . . and after seeing how much you've aged . . . and that day with the lightning . . . I guess it's just been a long morning. And a long night. I'm having a hard time comprehending all of this."

"I shouldn't think you have to comprehend it all now," said Franklin. "You have other more pressing matters."

"Yeah," Gerald replied uncertainly. He glanced down at his slumbering wife. "I'm afraid it's too late for some matters."

"Is it?" asked Franklin.

"There's been so much said." Gerald turned his eyes to the floor. "So much pain."

"A thing worth having is generally acquired through great pain," said Franklin.

"There are limits to how much pain anyone should have to endure," said Gerald. "My family has endured so much."

"Perhaps you should inquire of them whether they would prefer to endure it with you or without you."

Gerald nodded slowly.

Tory emerged shortly thereafter, his arm in a sling. Before they left the hospital, Gerald used the pay phone to call his boss in Chicago. He explained what had happened. He told him it would be impossible to fly to Dallas today or tomorrow. Gerald offered to fax him all the information so he could send another director. His boss was very disappointed. He knew this meant the sellers might go with another buyer.

"A week ago you told me that *nothing* would get in the way of this deal," his boss complained. "Nothing!"

"A week ago there wasn't anything that would have," Gerald replied. "Today I found something that will."

During the ride home, Franklin sat in the back seat with the two children. Tory still felt a little groggy. Michalene gripped Franklin's arm. Anytime Franklin wished to move, she was reluctant to let go.

Bonnie and Gerald sat up front. They spoke of the future. Neither of them was quite sure how to judge the change taking place in their hearts. It was too soon to dismiss the idea of a separation. Gerald's lease on his new apartment was for six months. Bonnie thought that might be enough time to decide. To Gerald, six months sounded like a century. But he accepted that he'd inflicted at least half of his family's pain—well, okay, three-fourths. Some very strong hints had now registered within him that his family was a prize worth winning, whether it took six months or six years.

As the Bonneville pulled into the Mickelsons' driveway, Franklin noticed storm clouds brewing on the horizon. After stepping out of the car, he paused to gaze at those clouds.

Michalene seemed to know what he was thinking. Tory knew it too. The philosopher watched and waited while Bonnie and Gerald went inside. It was only a few seconds before they glimpsed a faint bolt of lightning.

"You're gonna try it, aren't you?" asked Tory.

"I'm not sure I have a choice," said Franklin. "Unless you and your sister wish to arrange my funeral. If we are wrong about the lightning, that service may be yours to perform anyway."

For Michalene, this news was like a stab in the heart.

Franklin put his arm around her shoulders and continued to gaze off at the storm. He sighed. So many regrets. So much left undone. The criminals who had set fire to the Mickelsons' home were still at large. Franklin reached inside his back pocket. The hoax letter was still there. But of what use was that letter today? Though reaction to the letter might be considerable, it would not begin until the letter was printed. Until then, Tory's life was in peril. Michalene estimated that the storm would be overhead within an hour. Franklin wondered how he could possibly deter these criminals in so short a time. It was the drugs they wanted. Only by returning what Tory had stolen would they leave the Mickelson family alone.

Or perhaps there was another solution . . .

Franklin smiled. The solution was perfect! Now, if he could only set the wheels in motion . . .

• • •

"Hello?" said Franklin.

Tory corrected Franklin on how to use a telephone. "You talk into this part."

He spoke into the mouthpiece. "Yes, hello?"

Franklin held the business card that had been given to Bonnie by the fat man in sunglasses. Michalene had dialed the number.

"Who is this?" said the voice on the other end.

"Someone important to you, I should think," said Franklin. "I have in my possession something you desire very much."

"Yeah? And what might that be?" grumbled the voice.

"An item recently stolen from your place of residence."

The voice erupted into a flurry of profanity and threats. Franklin placed the phone back onto the receiver.

"Atrocious manners!" Franklin proclaimed. "We'll allow him a moment to ruminate."

A few seconds later, Franklin had Michalene dial the number again.

"Are you prepared to speak a little more civilly?" Franklin asked. "Or should I call on you later?"

"How do I know you got the kilos?"

"You might have asked me to deliver them to you in person last night," said Franklin, "instead of popping me so rudely on the head."

"Ahhh," said the voice. "Now I know who you are. That little maggot Giles Peck told me all about you. Muhammad Ali with the fists."

Franklin continued. "Now then, I am prepared to return your drugs without further incident."

"Tell me where you are," the voice demanded.

"Not so hasty," said Franklin. "There are certain conditions you must be willing to accept."

"Conditions? First I'll tell you *my* conditions! If you don't give me back those bricks I'll rip your—!"

Franklin hung up the phone again. "What an incorrigible fellow!"

A moment later, Franklin called him back a third time. "Sir, you *must* learn some common courtesy. Should we converse on some other occasion?"

"What are your conditions?" said the man, exasperated.

"Quite simple," said Franklin. "Near the house that you set ablaze last night runs a graveled road. About an eighth of a mile up this road is posted a yellow sign which reads 'Discharging of Firearms Prohibited Inside City Limits.' Do you know it?"

"I think I might have seen it," said the voice.

"In exactly sixty minutes, I will meet you at this sign and

return your contraband. That will be 3:30 P.M. If you are too early or too late, I will not come. If you attempt further assaults on the Mickelson family, I will not come. As I approach, you will see that I am carrying your items on my person. My only other condition is that after I return your stolen articles you shall allow me to depart unmolested. Do we understand one another?"

The man released a low laugh. "Sounds like you're smarter than I thought. All right. I'll be there. But if there are any tricks—any sign of cops, *anything!*—I'll kill you. I'll kill the kid. I'll wipe out that whole family!"

"There will be no need for violence, I assure you. One hour then." Franklin hung up the phone.

Tory and Michalene looked dumbfounded. Where did he think he was going to get two kilos of cocaine in one hour? Franklin did not offer an explanation. He instructed the children to find him some sort of a carrying case.

Franklin led Michalene back toward her bedroom. The smell of smoke still permeated much of the house. Bonnie and Gerald were busy in the living room assessing the damage. Two walls would have to be rebuilt, at least partially. The furniture and carpet would have to be replaced. Overall, they felt remarkably fortunate. Gerald noted that his favorite picture of little Carolyn had not been damaged.

Michalene dug through her closet and found an old TransWorld Airlines flight bag. Franklin asked her to fill the bag with various odds and ends to give it some bulk. She threw in a small tape recorder, a tiny 110 flash camera, a hair brush, a couple of paperback books, and several music tapes.

"Is this enough?" she asked Franklin.

"More than enough, I should think."

As an afterthought, Michalene prepared to throw in her travel-size chessboard. As she rolled the set over in her hands, she experienced keen feelings of sadness and regret. There was so much she had hoped she and Franklin might do together. She had dreamed of visiting Philadelphia and Washington, D.C., with Benjamin Franklin at her side as a kind of tour guide. She had hoped to learn everything that he could possibly teach her. Looking down at the chessboard, she realized she hadn't even played him a game of chess. With a heavy heart, she mentioned the idea.

Franklin smiled warmly. "I believe there is time. Why don't you arrange the pieces?"

Michalene unfolded the board and arranged the tiny magnetic chessmen. During the first several moves, she was understandably distracted, but winning wasn't the point for Michalene. For the rest of her life she would relish the memory of having actually played chess with one of America's founding fathers.

Franklin had once written an essay on the morals of chess and the valuable qualities of mind that were enhanced by playing. Shortly after the game commenced, he asked Michalene, "What comparisons do you feel one might draw between life and a game of chess?"

Michalene shrugged. "I'm not sure."

"For one, we must never allow ourselves to be discouraged by present appearances," said Franklin. "The game is so full of events; there is such a variety of turns in it. After careful contemplation, the means for extricating oneself from every difficulty will eventually present itself."

"If chess is like life," said Michalene, "how come I do so much better at one than I do at the other?"

"Keep playing the game, my dear child," said Franklin. "Keep playing the game." And then Franklin drew his brows together and considered his next words carefully. "I must tell you something, Michalene. A thought struck me earlier today. At first I was hesitant to express it, the concept being so foreign to my nature. It occurred to me as your father and brother sat upon the pipe, awaiting their rescuers. The events at the river were not played out the way I had first seen them. This led me to reconsider the other event I saw: that of the political rally in the year 2020. Although I do not conceive that this event will play itself out any differently, I must confess my own perceptions may have led me to misinterpret that which I saw.

"I remember clearly, there were four persons standing upon that platform at the back of the train. A man, a woman, and two children. In my prejudice, I naturally assumed the political candidate named Mickelson to be the man upon the platform. I did not consider for a moment that the candidate could be somebody else—that it could be the woman. But now, in retrospect, it seems to me there were subtle hints I should have noted. It was the *woman* who stood one step forward. It was the *woman* whose waves to the crowd were most enthusiastic. Forgive me, Michalene. I no longer believe it was your brother I saw upon that platform. I believe it was you."

Michalene looked dumbstruck. "I—I don't know what to say—"

"Say nothing," said Franklin. "There's nothing to celebrate. You have about three decades of intense work ahead of you. If you succeed, it will not have been me who brought you this success."

Michalene's heart welled up with a renewed and profound courage. She had known all along that they were wrong—those narrow-minded classmates and strangers. She just needed to hear it once from someone else's lips. At last her eyes filled with tears and she embraced Benjamin

Franklin. The Philadelphia philosopher had given her precisely the gift she had sought. The gift of possibilities.

• • •

Tory made Gerald and Bonnie aware of Franklin's plan. Moments later, everyone gathered at the bay window in Gerald's den. They looked out toward the dirt road and the distant sign which read "Discharging of Firearms Prohibited." Everyone nervously awaited the arrival of the emerald green Corvette. Franklin sat on the couch in Gerald's office with the TWA flight bag in his lap. Tory and Michalene remained close on either side of him.

The rumble of thunder loomed closer and closer. The pitter-patter of rain began against the window. Such sounds were music to Franklin's ears. The family was only mildly startled when the lightning rod atop the house was jolted. Everyone looked at Franklin, knowing now that he was fully to blame for this phenomenon. Franklin smiled and shrugged.

Minutes later, the emerald green Corvette appeared. Following Franklin's instructions to the letter, the men drove slowly down the dirt road until they reached the yellow sign. They stopped, the engine cut out, and the men behind the tinted windows waited.

"I must go now," said Franklin.

Michalene helped him to stand. From his back pocket Franklin drew out the hoax letter. He handed it to Bonnie.

"You must see that this is printed," said Franklin. "Although I believe that what I am about to do will ensure that your family will no longer suffer abuse at the hands of these men, it might be interesting to see how well this letter hinders such men from abusing anyone else in the future."

Bonnie unfolded the paper and started to read. She

looked back at Franklin, a puzzled expression on her face, wondering for an instant if the letter was authentic. He winked. He would let her come to that decision on her own.

The family followed Franklin to the front door. Bonnie and Gerald still didn't know quite what to make of this man. The presence of Benjamin Franklin in their lives was not a dream, and yet it didn't quite feel like reality either. It seemed on a different plane altogether. It would take a few days to clearly assess what had happened.

But for the children, Benjamin Franklin had become their closest friend. Yet it was more than a friend about to walk out that door and out of their lives forever. Tory and Michalene would have felt no different losing their guardian angel.

Each of the children gave Franklin a final embrace. Franklin whispered in Tory's ear, "You might do well to stay clear of pipes and rivers from now on."

"Okay," Tory promised and wiped his eyes discreetly.

In Michalene's ear Franklin whispered, "There are great things ahead for you, my dear girl. Just keep playing the game."

"I will," she whispered in return.

With the TWA flight bag in hand, Franklin opened the door. Before stepping out into the storm, he turned back to the Mickelson family and said, "If by and by some inventor perchance may duplicate the effects of my chamber, I shall expect you all to come to dinner at my home at 316–318 High Street, Philadelphia, Pennsylvania."

The children smiled a little.

Franklin turned around. As swiftly as a man of seventy-eight years could proceed, he walked out into the storm and made his way toward the front gate. The storm had not yet attained full strength. The response of the lightning was rather slow. He was grateful for this. He hurried through the gate and stepped out into the dirt road.

The two men in the Corvette noticed him immediately. They climbed out of the car. Franklin decided it was best to walk slowly. He held the flight bag out front, in clear view of the drug dealers. The Mickelson family watched anxiously through the bay window in Gerald's den.

Franklin drew closer and closer to the Corvette. The nearer he got, the more nervous he became. He looked up at the sky. *Anytime,* he said to himself. *Anytime at all.*

When he reached a distance of about ten yards, he stopped. The plan didn't seem to be working. Was his body no longer a lightning rod? What would these man do when they discovered that their precious kilos of cocaine were not in the bag? The men at the Corvette began walking toward him. The fat one placed his hand on the revolver in his jacket.

"All right," he said. "Just toss it over."

Franklin didn't move. *Now or never,* he thought.

The men halted, confused. What was wrong with this guy? "Are you deaf?" the fat man cried. "I said toss it over!"

Franklin glanced right and then left, as if he'd forgotten that his feeble body couldn't possibly attempt to run. The fat man had had enough. He pulled out the revolver and aimed it at a spot between the philosopher's eyes.

At that instant a magnificent bolt of lightning discharged from the clouds. Franklin was instantly engulfed in brilliant blue light. The drug dealers were thrown back. After landing on their seats, the men yanked off their sunglasses. In horror, they continued to watch the glowing shape of Benjamin Franklin. The bright blue light swelled and contracted. And then the shape exploded. The body of Benjamin Franklin became like a sparkler on the Fourth of July.

Appendages of electrical fire shot out in all directions. The men shielded their eyes.

And then the light and the fire disappeared altogether, leaving only a quiet, empty road. After they had recovered, the drug dealers rushed over to the spot where Benjamin Franklin had been standing. The old man was gone! There was nothing left of him! Not even a scrap of clothing or a pile of ashes. The flight bag had also disappeared. The two kilos of cocaine! Like the old man, their fortunes had vanished into thin air.

Another bolt of lightning ignited the sky, followed by a rumble of vengeful thunder. The drug dealers scrambled back to their vehicle. They had no desire to be roasted and disintegrated in a similar manner.

As the Corvette sped away, Tory and Michalene mingled their tears with cheers. Their guardian angel had saved them once more.

And from that time forth, whenever lightning filled the skies of Illinois, the Mickelsons would come together and watch the display with tender appreciation, remembering well what the lightning had brought them one week during the rainy summer of 1993. And they also wondered if someday the lightning might bring back to their midst a certain philosopher from Philadelphia, Pennsylvania.

• • •

Floating, hovering, his body trembling, his veins boiling, the sensations of cold and hot washing over him successively, Franklin watched the colors blur and blend, sweep one direction and then the other and then a hundred different directions at once. Like an arrow piercing the veil of eternity, Benjamin Franklin flew across the field of time and space to a destiny unknown.

233

At last came the impact, like a hammer on an anvil. The wind expelled from Franklin's lungs. He bounced in the air. His body landed softly on the strangely alternating ground.

Franklin watched the sun and moon chase each other back and forth across the sky like a pair of playful lovers. Before the sky came to rest and before the universe stood still, he once again saw visions in the quivering of time. And then the face of Benjamin Franklin became radiant with wonder.

It was not 1790. Nor was it Philadelphia. Nor was it like any place Franklin could have ever imagined . . .